Will You
Catch Me?

Will You Catch Me?

JANE ELSON

Hodder Children's Books
An imprint of
Hachette Children's Group
Part of Hodder and Stoughton
Carmelite House
50 Victoria Embankment
London EC4Y 0DZ

An Hachette Company
www.hachette.co.uk

Hodder
Children's
Books

HODDER CHILDREN'S BOOKS

First published in Great Britain in 2018 by Hodder and Stoughton

1 3 5 7 9 10 8 6 4 2

Text copyright © Jane Elson, 2018

A CIP catalogue record for this book
is available from the British Library.

ISBN 978 1 444 92778 8

Typeset in Egyptian 505 by Avon DataSet Ltd,
Bidford-on-Avon, Warwickshire

Printed and bound in Great Britain by Clays Ltd, Elcograf S.p.A.

The paper and board used in this book
are made from wood from responsible

www.hachettechildrens.co.uk

This book is written in memory of
Viola Clarke
11th July 1928 – 19th July 2016
Who sailed from Jamaica to England,
arriving on these shores
on the 2nd of February 1952,
Beloved mother of Sharon D. Clarke MBE
& Aunty Vie to us all.
We love you and miss you and were so blessed to
have you in our lives.

'There can be no keener revelation of a society's soul than the way in which it treats its children.'

Nelson Mandela

'It takes a village to raise a child.'

African proverb

For my Dad, Brian Elson, who as a boy saved his jam jars of sticklebacks, newts and tadpoles, two at a time, as Hitler's bombs were falling and my grandma was screaming at him to get in the air raid shelter.

naturalist definition
a person who studies plants, animals, insects and other living things.

In the Beginning

In the beginning there was just me and Mum, then the demon drink came and took her over like a shadow, and our family became me and Mum and drink.

But before the demon drink came into our lives, she would tell me bedtime stories about Noah saving the animals two by two, and how he lived on an ark with his animal family (as well as his human family), to save them all from the flood.

Noah must have been a very nice man and a naturalist to save all those animals. He made me realise I needed an animal family too. So I started to save animals from people who didn't want them any more, starting with Bob Marley my tortoise, who I found wandering all alone on the wasteland, the scrubby grass next to my estate. I am the only naturalist on the Beckham Estate which makes me unique.

In the beginning our family was just me and Mum, then it became me, Mum, demon drink and my animal family.

My name is Nell Hobs and this is my story.

1

Standing on my head at one o'clock in the morning makes the world seem a better place. My deepest fears vanish as the blood rushes to my brain. It stops me thinking scary thoughts like, WHERE IS MY MUM?

The world looks better when you're upside down, it's a fact.

When I stand on my head in the playground at school, the other kids' faces look blurry – my eyes hit their chins first and nobody looks pretty, not even Chantal Smith. It makes me giggle. We're all equal upside down. At this exact moment I am standing on my head in my bedroom, with my feet against the wall, and scatter cushions spread around me for a safe crash landing. I like the shapes and night shadows of upside-down furniture much better than right-way-up tables and chairs and wardrobes.

But if I'm going to be truthful with you, like no word of a lie, the main reason I stand on my head is because when the blood rushes to my brain, I can forget my issues like:

1. The dad issue, as in, I don't have one and Mum won't tell me who he is
2. Where's Mum, and why isn't she home yet?

I'm not good at sleeping when I've got anxieties.

When I was a little kid, Mum used to say this nursery rhyme to me every night to get me to sleep:

Ride a cock-horse to Banbury Cross,
To see a fine lady upon a white horse,
Rings on her fingers and bells on her toes,
She shall have music wherever she goes.

I slept well when I was a little kid.

One of my curls is itching my nose. I try my best to ignore it but I can't. I push my feet against the wall and crash land on my scatter cushions. Scrambling up, I stare in the mirror at my pale as marble face, now flushed from my headstand, my deep brown eyes and wild black curls.

Aunty Lou says it's a good thing the Lord brought her from Jamaica to London England, to live next door to me on the Beckham Estate, so she can keep an eye on me and comb my knotty-knotty hair.

She always mutters under her breath, 'Nell STAND STILL,' and attacks my tangles with a comb. My eyes water just thinking about it. Michael, Aunty Lou's nephew, who lives with her, always laughs at me when she catches me with the comb. He's my best friend now that I don't talk to Chantal Smith any more.

I look at the tin can hanging on a hook by my window and consider waking up Michael so we can talk.

The walkie-talkie Michael made is genius. He made it from two empty baked bean cans. The string from my can goes out through the window, along the back wall between our flats and in through Michael's bedroom window, where his baked bean can also hangs on a hook.

I've got anxieties tonight but I don't think I should bother Michael at two minutes past one in the morning. It doesn't seem fair.

Aunty Lou would go mental if she knew Mum

hadn't come home . . . and that she's out most nights.

So I made Michael promise not to tell.

We made our *No Word of a Lie Promise*, linking thumbs. I save my linking little fingers pinkie promise just for my mum.

'I *No Word of a Lie Promise* that I won't tell Aunty Lou unless there's an emergency,' said Michael, 'and the code word is . . . ?'

'*Operation Ark*,' I decide.

'*Operation Ark*,' he agreed. 'Nell, you gotta promise to use our code word if you need help,' and we hatched our emergency plan, huddled together on a winter evening, whispering our secrets into the cold night air.

I snatch up my silver charm bracelet Mum gave me for my birthday from my bedside table. It's my most precious possession. I run the miniature Noah, ark, and all the tiny silver animals through my fingers. My favourite are the two giraffes.

There's a clattering at the window and my heart literally stops for a zillionth of a second, 'cause I think it's Mum, but it's not – it's Napoleon, the enormous ginger cat, an unofficial part of my animal family. He's called Napoleon on account of the fact

4

that he invades whichever flat he pleases on the Beckham Estate and takes it over.

I open my window and let him in. He leaps on to my knee as I sit on my bed, and I bury my hand into his lovely, warm ginger fur. Stroking him calms me down a bit.

I love Napoleon and I think he loves me, but mostly he likes to sit on my knee, licking his lips, looking at the other members of my animal family.

And it's grown into a big family. Let me introduce you:

1. Margaret and Mable are my Abyssinian guinea pigs. They're, no word of a lie, the cheekiest, cutest guinea pigs I've ever seen in my life. Margaret's coat is brindle, a mixture of red and black, and Mable's coat is cream. Mum had a job cleaning in a florist for a while and she found the guinea pigs, abandoned with the dead roses in a cardboard box by the bins. At this moment they're huddled together having a little nap in their cage. Most of

the time they chat squeaks to me, even at night WHEN I AM TRYING TO SLEEP.

2. Aunty Lou is my Syrian hamster, called after my favourite aunty, though she doesn't know it yet. She's the newest member of my animal family. The people in the flat above us were getting evicted and Michael and I were having a nose. I heard the hamster wheel squeaking as it went round, through the open door.

'I'm a naturalist,' I said to the scary-looking bailiffs, as I dodged past them to rescue the hamster. When I carried the hamster cage out on to the balcony, a lady with a shaved head and an eagle tattoo on her arm was outside smoking a cigarette and crying.

'Have the little pest,' she said to me. 'It gets on my nerves.'

Michael and I took turns to carry the cage back down to my flat.

3. Beyoncé and Destiny are my Oranda goldfish. With the fancy bobbles on their heads and their stunning fanned tails,

they swim round their bowl like divas with sass and attitude. They belonged to old Mrs Simonds, from Aunty Lou's church. She sadly died and Aunty Lou knew that Mrs Simonds would be very happy knowing that a naturalist was looking after her goldfish.

4. Bob Marley is my Hermann's tortoise and the first member of my animal family. Michael and I found him on the wasteland wandering along happy as can be. Michael and I put *Found Tortoise* posters everywhere, with a handsome photograph of Bob Marley. We even took him down to the vets to see if he was microchipped, but he wasn't, so finders keepers, I reckoned.

Aunty Lou named him after her favourite singer from Jamaica and she said that, 'Bob Marley's one chilled-out tortoise.' Michael and I had a naming ceremony, with a feast of jerk chicken, toasting my new tortoise with my most favourite drink, mango juice.

5. Fiz and Tyrone are my gerbils. Some cruel person actually left them in a cage, in the rain, just dumped by the road, where anything could've happened to them. They're named after two characters from *Coronation Street*, which I watch with Mum. We snuggle up on the sofa together, with mugs of tea and something to eat – that's if Mum's remembered to go to the shops. On the windowsill, living in jam jars, are the other beasts and bugs that I rescue from the Beckham Estate and Parliament Hill Fields who just, shall we say, stay the night in Nell's Bed and Breakfast to recover before I set them free the next day.

In Nell's Bed and Breakfast tonight ARE:
Caterpillars x2 (rescued with a zillionth of a second to spare from a bush that the council were about to trim.)

Woodlouse x1 (crawling along our balcony not looking very happy. They eat rotten wood. The balcony's made of metal. It must have been hungry.)

Newt x1 (that didn't look as if it could swim very well.)

Spider x1 (It got trapped in Michael's school locker with his smelly trainers, poor thing!)

On my bookcase, the shelves are rammed full of copies of my favourite magazine *Creepy Crawly Fact or Fiction*, which tells me interesting facts like:

If you weighed all the insects in the world they would weigh more than all the humans in the world. Which means that there are more insects living in Kentish Town than humans. Thank goodness there's only one Chantal Smith.

My magazines on the top shelf are propped up against my purple jar with *Ark Fund* painted on the side which I decorated in junior school. Aunty Lou sometimes gives me money for helping her tidy up for my animal family food fund, and Mum gives me pocket money when she remembers. I need every penny to feed my animal family.

The sound of a key in the lock makes my heart jump. Napoleon hisses and sticks his claws through my PJ trousers as he leaps into the air and vanishes under my bed.

I run into the hall as the front door bangs open, and Mum falls through it on to the welcome door mat. A man with a tangled beard and dirty jeans and T-shirt falls through after her and they laugh as they clutch at the walls and heave themselves up, only it's not funny and my happiness to see her smashes into a thousand pieces.

'SHHHHHHHHHH, you'll wake Nell,' says Mum.

'I am already awake, Mum.'

Mum peers at me through smeared mascara. 'Oh, there you are my Nelly nell nell. This is Baz.'

'He's not my dad, is he?'

And my mum and Baz laugh hard at me as they stagger into the front room and then slam the door.

A tear splashes off the end of my nose. I hadn't even realised my eyes were leaking. Wiping my face on my PJ sleeve I go back to bed, pulling my quilt over my head. I try to sleep but I can't, so I do a headstand on my bed.

I hear Baz's growly voice say, 'Casey, come here,' as they stumble back into the hall.

'Stacey,' she says, giggling. 'My name's Stacey.'

Then there's shuffling and the front door slams.

I hear Baz staggering along outside, kicking a can, singing that football song about not walking alone at the top of his voice. I hear windows and doors banging open and people swearing and someone shouts, 'SHUT UP!'

Michael's muffled voice comes from the walkie-talkie by the window.

'*Nell, are you receiving? Aunty Lou has woken and is on her way to you. Operation Ark to commence. I repeat, Operation Ark to commence.*'

With wobbly legs I walk to the window and speak into the tin can, '*Receiving over and out.*'

Three loud knocks on the kitchen window make me jolt from my bones. I walk with dread steps towards the kitchen.

Time to put *Operation Ark* into action.

2

The kitchen door's open, the light on. Mess and chaos everywhere. I jump as I see Aunty Lou, lit by the dim street light on the Beckham Estate, staring through the window, dressed in her pink bath robe with a scarf wrapped round her head. Michael is peering over her shoulder, in his dressing gown and PJs, torch in hand.

I tiptoe into the kitchen. Mum's slumped over the table, asleep, an empty wine glass tipped over next to her. Her pale skin is flushed, her golden hair fanning over the table.

I check she's still breathing. I'm always doing that.

I get a bowl from under the sink and put it next to her on the table in case she's sick.

I push the pile of dirty, smelly plates aside and climb up to kneel on the draining board, fiddling with the window catch till it opens. I heave the window up and shiver as the night air creeps in.

'Nell, child, you're not staying here tonight. Open the front door and let me in, please. And, Nell, put your dressing gown and slippers on, you'll catch your death.'

'The front door's locked, Aunty Lou, I'll try to find the key,' I say.

I climb down from the draining board and run into my bedroom, wriggling into my purple, fluffy dressing gown and pushing my tiny feet into my big, furry tarantula slippers that are lying under my bed.

I scurry around, looking in all the places Mum might've put the key. Mum has this thing, however out of it she is, about locking the front door from the inside to keep us safe. Only it doesn't keep me safe. It keeps me and my animal family trapped. I run back into the kitchen and climb back on to the draining board.

'It's no good. I've looked for the front door key in all Mum's usual places.' I say.

TJ, Aunty Lou's son, appears at the window, pulling a white T-shirt over his head.

'What's happening, Nell?' He grins at me, rubbing

his eyes at the same time. Then he sees Mum and his smile vanishes.

'Nell's coming home with us,' says Aunty Lou. 'Help her out of the window, TJ.'

'No, Aunty Lou, not without my animal family. They've got to come too.'

'What's this foolishness? It's the middle of the night. We need to get you into bed,' says Aunty Lou.

'You said families stick together and they *are* my family,' I say.

'Please, Nell, I'm begging you, just come next door, so we can all get some sleep. Your animals will be fine. You'll see them in the morning.'

I shake my head.

'I'll buy you some sweets, anything you want, just come next door please.'

'You can't bribe me, Aunty Lou, families stick together, they're coming with—'

'Yeah, we gotta do Operation Ark, like Noah did in the Bible,' says Michael, 'we've planned it.'

'Oh, you've *planned it*, have you?' says Aunty Lou.

'Yes, we rescue the animals two by two,' I say.

'Into my bedroom,' adds Michael.

Aunty Lou looks from me to Michael and back to

me again, and slowly a smile lights up her face. She holds her hands up to heaven.

'Well, if Noah can do it, so can we.'

'Let's get on with it. Morning's coming,' says TJ.

'We'll do the guinea pigs first,' I say to Michael. He nods and disappears next door.

'Lead the way,' TJ says when he's climbed through the window.

So I take them to my room and we start to move the animals like Noah did – only it's not always two by two, 'cause Bob Marley my tortoise and Aunty Lou hamster keep their own company.

'You've got a proper zoo here, Nell.' TJ squeezes my shoulder. 'That tortoise table won't go through the window, no way. We'll have to make do at ours.'

I open the cage, grab Mable and give her to TJ. The little cream guinea pig nestles into his neck.

'I'll take Margaret,' I say, 'she's the noisiest.' And true to my words she starts doing guinea pig chat at the top of her squeaky voice.

We carry the squirming guinea pigs into the kitchen and hand them through the window to Aunty Lou and to Michael, who has returned and has a box waiting for them. He then takes this back to his flat.

Then TJ and I go back for the guinea pig cage. It's heavy and digs into my hands as we carry the cage through to the kitchen. We lift it up on to the draining board and ease it through the kitchen window, where Michael and Aunty Lou are waiting again.

Beyoncé and Destiny are next, my diva red Oranda goldfish, with their fanned-out tails and fins, which make them look like they have fancy dresses on – the kind you'd wear to the Oscars. TJ carries them in their heavy goldfish bowl, being careful not to slosh the water.

Napoleon, the ginger cat, is waiting on the draining board, licking his lips.

'Out of the way, Napoleon,' I order. He ignores me.

TJ rests Beyoncé and Destiny on the kitchen table and tries to grab Napoleon, who spits at him and jumps out of the window.

Through the window go Beyoncé and Destiny to Aunty Lou, who holds the bowl just while TJ climbs back out of the kitchen window, so he can then take my goldfish into Aunt Lou's flat.

As soon as Beyoncé and Destiny are safe, I run to get Bob Marley, who's so chilled, he's not at all bothered about being handed through the kitchen window at two in the morning. I think he secretly enjoys the excitement only he's too cool to show it.

I grab some rocks and handfuls of beech chippings from my tortoise table, shove them in a bag, and pass them through the window so that Bob Marley can be comfortable for the night.

I go back to my bedroom for my hamster so I can pass the cage to Aunty Lou, who shudders.

'What's this? I haven't met this one before?'

'We rescued her from the flat above,' I say. 'I've called her Aunty Lou.'

'I don't want some ratty-ratty thing called after me, thank you very much,' says Aunty Lou.

'She's not a rat. She's a Syrian hamster,' I say in my best most patient voice. 'I named my favourite hamster after my favourite aunty.'

Aunty Lou doesn't look impressed, but I reckon my hamster likes her name Aunty Lou, so Aunty Lou it is and I reckon human Aunty Lou is secretly pleased, only she doesn't show it.

I grab Fizz and Tyrone's gerbilarium, and hand it through the window.

Then back and forth back and forth I go with the

other beasts and bugs staying in Nell's Bed and
Breakfast

Caterpillars x2

Woodlouse x1

Newt x1

And lastly the spider I rescued from Michael's
locker. And do you know what, through all of that cat
spitting, talking and guinea pig chat, Mum didn't
even stir once.

I shove food for my animals in a laundry bag and
hand it through the window to Michael.

'Come on, Nell,' whispers Aunty Lou.

'I got to put Mum to bed,' I say.

'No, Nell, that's not your job. She's the adult.
When she wakes she'll put herself to bed.' She fishes
the Post-it notes and pen she always has with her
from her dressing gown pocket and writes:

Nell and zoo at ours,
Lou

She reaches through the window and slaps it on
the wall.

'Just a minute,' I say.

I run back to my bedroom and grab my quilt and

18

my favourite turquoise scatter cushion.

I put the quilt around Mum's shoulders, ease the cushion under her head and kiss her on her soft cheek. I rummage in the bits and bobs drawer for the box of headache tablets, and I fill a glass full of water and put it near her hand, so she can drink it in the morning to make her feel better.

'Bye, Mum,' I whisper into her ear, 'I love you.' But she doesn't hear. She never does when the demon drink has her.

Michael helps me settle my animal family into his room for the night.

Margaret and Mable are doing guinea pig chat from the box balanced on Michael's bed.

'We need to make room for their cage,' says Michael, as he stumbles over it.

I run over to help Michael move a big box that has *Invention for Operation Ark* written on the side.

'What's that?' I ask.

I can see that he has started to build a shelf around the walls of the room.

'You'll see,' says Michael, tapping the side of his nose.

The hiss and sweet smell of frying plantains wafts

down the hall. My tummy rumbles. All my anxieties had squashed hunger out of my brain.

Aunty Lou calls, 'Nell, come.'

'You'd best go,' says Michael. 'I'll sort out Margaret and Mable.'

I walk with dread steps into the kitchen to Aunty Lou.

'Tell me the truth. Did your mum put any food in your belly before she went out tonight?'

I shake my head. My betrayal of Mum slices through me but I'm so, so hungry.

'Sit,' says Aunty Lou, pulling out a chair for me at the kitchen table. She hands me a fish finger and fried plantain sandwich on hard dough bread with a cup of mango juice. I take a gigantic greedy piglet bite of sandwich, to avoid the questions that I know are coming.

But Aunty Lou waits for me to swallow my mouthful.

'Look at me, Nell. Has your mum been leaving you on your own at night?'

My eyes prickle and it comes out as barely a whisper of betrayal. 'Sometimes.'

'And that no good worthless man who woke up half the estate, has she done that before?'

I shake my head. 'No.'

Aunty Lou takes my chin in her hands and tilts it so I'm looking in her eyes.

'Truth,' she says.

'Not for the longest time. Not since I was little. I used to pour them drinks when she brought people home.'

Aunty Lou takes me in her arms and hold me so tight.

Michael comes running in with the empty cardboard box in one hand, clutching Mable in the other.

'Margaret's escaped,' he says.

Panic swallows me and before I know it Aunty Lou, TJ, Michael and I are running round like mad people. Aunty Lou's on her hands and knees under the kitchen table and I'm trying to look behind the cooker when I hear a rustling coming from Aunty Lou's baking cupboard.

Aunty Lou hears it too and bumps her head as she comes out from under the table.

'I think she's in the kitchen,' I call and TJ and Michael run in just as I open the cupboard door and a walking snowball comes waddling out. It's Margaret, covered head to toe in flour. An empty packet of self-raising flour topples out behind her. There's flour everywhere.

Mable is squealing as she's so excited to see her friend.

Aunty Lou puts her hands over her ears. 'I am renaming those guinea pigs Asbo and Chaos.'

ASBO means Anti-Social Behaviour Order. Finn, who lives on the eleventh floor, had one when he was younger, before he started playing the guitar. 'I love those names,' I say, 'Asbo and Chaos.'

We all start laughing and cannot stop. Probably because we're all stupid with tiredness.

'We have to have one of our naming ceremonies then,' says Michael, 'it's the law.' And he starts making us all hot chocolate.

When we all have a mug in our hand I say, 'I name these guinea pigs Asbo and Chaos,' in my best, most solemn voice, and we all clink mugs.

Aunty Lou finds me an old brush and places a towel over my lap, so I can get the flour out of Margaret— I mean Asbo's coat. 'I'll sort your cupboard, Aunty Lou,' I say. 'Sorry for Asbo's disruptive behaviour.'

'No, I'll sort out my baking cupboard in the morning,' she says closing the door on the mess.

'Now bed, all of you before the birds start singing. Tomorrow is a big day. Michael and I are going to see his dad after school. He's working in town and staying the night in a hotel and we're going to stay with him.'

'I could stay with TJ,' mumbles Michael.

'Your father's made this effort and we will oblige him. He wants to see you, his son Michael.'

'It'll be nice to see your dad, Michael,' I say, but he bites his lip and won't look at me.

'TJ,' says Aunty Lou. 'Will you check up on Nell tomorrow?'

TJ winks at me. 'Yes, Mum.'

And as we play with Asbo and Chaos and finish our hot chocolates down to the last little drop, I look round at these kind people, who are like precious treasures in my life, and think of all the bother I have caused them.

I simply have to find my dad.

3

It was a blackbird's song that woke me.

Aunty Lou turns over in her sleep and mumbles. I wriggle out from under the covers on the camp bed.

My eyes are gritty with tiredness. I look around for my school stuff, then with a silent groan I realise my school uniform and books are still next door. I'll have to go home to get them.

I have a lot to do before school. Firstly, I've got to feed and water my animal family and give them some love. I go down the hallway and squash my ear to Michael's door. I hear the whirring and the clicking of all the half-working clocks that Michael likes to take to pieces. I open the door and peep round; he's sprawled asleep on the bed, one leg and arm hanging over the side. His canerow hair is peeping out from under a pillow. I creep in.

On the bed lies a silver-framed photograph of Michael's mum and dad, hugging and smiling in the sunshine. Michael's mum's mind got sick and she just got so sad she didn't know how to live her life any more, so she's being cared for in Jamaica, and his dad's busy all the time, but Michael don't like to talk about it. He must've fallen asleep looking at his mum and dad. I place the photo back on his bedside table.

I can't help myself and tickle the bottom of Michael's foot.

'GERRR OFFF,' he growls, throwing his pillow at me.

'Michael, you gotta get up.' I shake his shoulder.

'I'm two months and three days older than you, stop bossing me about.' He turns over and goes back to sleep.

Margaret and Mable, sorry I mean Asbo and Chaos, greet me with guinea pig chat.

I set to work feeding my family from my laundry bag store. I make sure they all have plenty of fresh water.

I go to TJ's room to see Bob Marley, who spent the night there. The door's open, the bed empty. He must've gone to college really early.

Bob Marley is chilling on his tortoise rock in his makeshift pen which TJ has made out of the broken wardrobe door lying on its side and a wall of shoe boxes that TJ keeps his best trainers in. The wardrobe door has a Post-it stuck to it with Aunty Lou's handwriting.

> Michael, you are in big trouble, do not take screws from door hinges. **THE DOOR FALLS OFF!** Wardrobes are for hanging clothes in and not, I repeat, **NOT FOR YOUR INVENTIONS.**

Aunty Lou says she believes that *a written telling off is there for eternity, as a reminder of the misdeed.* This is why she sticks Post-its everywhere.

I feed Bob Marley and top up the baking tray TJ's filled with water for my tortoise to drink and have a dip in.

I spy a scribbled note on top of the chest of drawers.

> Morning, Nell, Bob Marley and me are now brothers! Respect due to your little tortoise man. Leave your animals with us till we know what's happening with your mum.
>
> TJ x

It's good to see TJ taking an interest in reptiles.

'Be good, Bob Marley,' I say, and go back to Michael's room. He's still sleeping. I pull his quilt off him and shout in his ear, 'MICHAEL, GET UP FOR SCHOOL!'

'Go away, Nell,' he mutters, turning over again.

'Bet I get to school before you,' I whisper in his ear. But then guilt tickles my conscience – it's my fault he's had no sleep.

I open his bedroom window and set free the spider and woodlouse from my jam jars, and I check on the rainwater-filled tank of tadpoles we keep on Michael's window sill. When we planned *Operation Ark*, we thought it would be too much for them. So this is their permanent home. I mash up some of Aunty Lou's left-over green peas from the kitchen, and feed them. A group of frogs is called an army. I wish I could march to school with an army of frogs to protect me from lessons like boring history with Miss Radlett.

I take a last look at my animal family. All's fine.

I tip Michael's grandad's old brown leather briefcase that he uses for school upside down, until I find a pen, then I tear the back page out of his maths book and write:

> Michael, please take my newt and release him in the ponds on Parliament Hill on the way to school. Please release my caterpillars on to a nice tree, so they have good leaves to eat.
> Nell

I take a deep breath. Now to check on Mum.

I feel a spring breeze rustle my hair as I go out of the front door in my purple dressing gown and tarantula slippers. Through the window I see Mum, still slumped over the kitchen table. My quilt's fallen on to the kitchen floor. She's so still. My heart stops.

I bang on the window and am so relieved when she sits bolt upright, smiles her dazzling smile, then slumps back over and goes back to sleep.

'Mum,' I shout, 'you've got to let me in. I've got to get dressed for school. MUM.'

I end up having to wriggle back through the window. When I get into the kitchen, I shake Mum's shoulder. 'Mum, please, let me get you into bed.'

'Nell, I love you,' she says, waking and putting her arm round me, but she smells of wine.

'I love you too, Mum,' I say, 'but you need to go to sleep in your bed, not on the kitchen table.'

I somehow haul her up, knocking the chair over, which crashes the pedal bin on its side in the process. I help her to her bedroom, which takes ages as her legs keep getting tangled with mine, and although Mum's skinny she's somehow really heavy.

I flop her on to the bed, and as I look down at her pretty face, spoilt with red scaly patches, spots and lines on her forehead, panic fills me from head to toe. I don't care that I've promised not to ask her about my dad. I need him.

'My Nell,' Mum mumbles. 'Always looking after me like a good girl.' She lifts up her head and reaches out her hand to me, the hand with *Pinkie* tattooed on the little finger.

'Mum.' My words tiptoe with caution. 'I was thinking last night, when you were out so late . . . if I had a dad then he could look after me when you're not home.'

'Oh, Nell,' Mum says with a sigh.

'Who is he? Please, why won't you tell me?'

'Nell, you're giving me a headache.' Mum puts her arm over her eyes. 'Just – shut up about your dad.'

The kick of her words boils my blood.

'No, I won't shut up. You need to find him and

see if he might want to live with us. You won't know if you don't try! Or maybe if he's got a family somewhere else, I can go and stay with them when you're too busy drinking to care about me.'

'Nell!' Mum darts upright.

'Well, it's true – if you cared about me you would stop!'

And before Mum can even answer, I run out of the room and slam the door on my way out.

'Nell,' she calls but I ignore her. I go into the kitchen and see my turquoise cushion on the kitchen floor. My most favourite cushion has a dribble mark on it. I scrub the stained bit under the tap and take it to my bedroom, turn the damp bit towards the floor and stand on my head, looking around my upside-down bedroom. Mum's still calling out for me, but I still ignore her.

My birth certificate's blank under *Father*. I saw it once, a long time ago, when I was snooping round Mum's bedroom. I don't know where it is now. Mum's not good with documents. But somewhere in number six Beckham Estate must be a clue as to who my dad is and I need to find it. I drag on my school trousers, shirt and tie and then head back into the kitchen. A toilet roll tube, baked bean can and screwed-up piece of paper have tipped out of the fallen pedal bin, so I shove them back in but then I catch sight of an x on the paper. I fish it from the bin and smooth it out. Water's been spilt on it and it's smudged and hard to read. I don't recognise the handwriting.

It's got a kiss and a promise. I know it's only a screwed-up bit of paper with a kiss on but it means someone's been in my flat, promising a kiss to my mum, and my imagination flies into a fantasy of my dad visiting Mum in secret when I am not there. This might be my first clue.

I find my khaki school rucksack behind the sofa. Mum bought it for me for Christmas. It's just like the ones naturalists in Africa wear on their backs, when they track lions and elephants. I put my possible clue safely in one of the zip-up pockets.

I look in the kitchen for something to take to school for lunch but the cupboards are empty.

Mum should be out looking for a new job after getting fired from the baker's last month but who's going to give her a job in this state.

'Nell, Nell!' shouts Mum.

I can't ignore her any more so I go into her bedroom and look down at her.

'Mum, when you've had a sleep you should get dressed.'

'I *pinkie promise*,' says Mum, wiggling her finger with the tattoo.

'*Pinkie promise*,' I say and we link little fingers with love.

4

By the time I've left the flat I'm so late, but I'm not the only one. I see Michael running ahead of me and I remember my bet.

But Michael soon disappears and my legs and brain are too tired to try to beat him so I decide to walk to school.

1. It will increase my chances of seeing wildlife.
2. Chantal Smith is probably on the bus.

Chantal and I used to be friends, only she kept wanting to come round to my flat and I just couldn't have her there, not with my mum the way she is, so I started ignoring her and now she hates me. I missed her friendship, till Michael came to live at Aunty Lou's. He's a much better friend, but it makes me sad that I can't have sleepovers like other girls.

My journeys to school are like safaris through North West London. I adjust my rucksack on to my shoulders and set off on my travels.

A flock of pigeons flies overhead in search of food in the savage urban landscape. One lands on a piece of newspaper lying on the pavement, flapping in the breeze. His wing hangs at a strange angle. He looks as if he's been picked on by the other pigeons. Mother Nature can be cruel. I walk forwards slowly to rescue him, but he flies off, over the silver birch trees. I pick up the newspaper to put it in the bin as it's important for us naturalists to look after our environment. It's a torn page from *North West London Tonight* with a picture of the mayor, Felicity Cordour, with her blonde wavy hair, smiling up at me. The headline says, *Celebrate Heritage Day with King Charles the Second*. Then it says *animal lover Mayor Felicity*. But I can't read the rest as it's ripped so I put it in the bin.

I continue my safari past the overflowing bins. A black tom cat with one ear emerges from the tallest bin with his prey in his mouth. It's actually a piece of half-eaten Kentucky Fried Chicken. Urban prey is different from the prey that big cats eat in Africa.

A pug makes its weary way to the waterhole (the puddle by the bus stop). I watch as he laps up the much-needed water but in a moment he is whisked up by his owner and put in a stupid pink handbag. This would also never happen in Africa.

When I reach the forbidden short cut through the fence, behind the old girls' changing rooms, I crawl on my hands and knees through the grass. I stop and look at the wild daisies, dandelions and some early daffodils coming through. Two ladybirds are nestled in one daffodil, which is rare. One has seven spots, the other has four. Lucy Cooke, my most favourite presenter off the TV, would be impressed. I'm anxious that the ladybirds will be trampled on by kids escaping from school. I hold out my fingers; one crawls on to my left hand, the other on to my right, and now I'm going to be even later for school as I have to walk slowly, to make sure my ladybird friends don't get squashed, because that would be a tragedy.

I always need to check behind the old girls' changing rooms for wildlife. I found a fox at school last November, cowering with an injured paw. Some year nine boys were shouting at it and Kyle from my year seven class even threw a Coke can at it. No word of a lie, anger set me on fire and I ran towards them screaming, 'Leave the fox alone!' The boys actually scarpered. Michael reckons it's because they saw Mr Richardson the head teacher in the distance but I think it's 'cause they were scared of me.

I stayed with the frightened fox to protect him, while Michael ran and got my favourite teacher, Miss Petunia. She teaches us biology and she let me use her phone to call the Mr Tod Fox Sanctuary and also to take photos to document the rescue when the lady from the sanctuary came to collect the fox. I hope the fox is happy now.

To my relief, today there is no injured wildlife behind the old girls' changing rooms.

I've definitely missed registration, but a naturalist has duties. I walk past the Thinking Room – where you're sent if you need time out – and then the school hall, which got flooded last September. They had to cancel the Welcome to Year Seven parents' evening at the end of the first term because of the hall. My class cheered when it was cancelled, which was stupid, because now it's been rescheduled for the middle of this term, which means the teachers have a term and a half's stuff to moan to the parents about, rather than just one term. Still,

I hope Mum remembers to come.

The school hall smells fusty still. I hear the workmen banging around inside. When I reach the office, Miss Gordon tuts. 'Late again.'

'I gotta go to history,' I mutter and rush off, before she starts asking questions.

The school don't know about my mum, and I get such anxieties that they will guess. Aunty Lou says that as long as I am living next door, she can keep an eye on me.

I once heard her say to Mum, 'Stacey, I believe that somewhere inside you you have the strength to stop drinking.' But after last night, I don't know what Aunty Lou's thinking, which makes me want to stand on my head, but I have reached my history class.

Miss Radlett, our history teacher, is so strict and I hate history and her groaning on about DEAD PEOPLE AND BORING BATTLES.

I take a deep breath and push the classroom door open.

But Miss Radlett's not there. In her place stands a smiling man. 'Hello, I am Mr Samuels and you are . . .?'

'Nell, sir, Nell Hobs.'

Everything about him is a little bit faded: his grey

jumper, his hair – a little bit greying – his trousers made of that corduroy old people wear, even his smile, that makes his lips and eyes dance.

'Please, sir,' I say. 'Where's Miss Radlett?'

'She's got stress,' shouts out Michael, who's grinning at me from the back. 'Ha, beat you to school, Nell.' He nods to a place next to him.

'Miss Radlett's taking some time away from you lot, so you have to put up with me,' says Mr Samuels.

His register is lying on the desk, open. I point to my name and he ticks it off. Even his biro has faded ink.

My ladybird friends are tickling my fingers; they must like my hands as they haven't flown off.

The Beckham Street Boyz from our estate sit on the right, and the T Crew from the Tarkey House Estate sit on the left. It's just the way it is.

Chantal Smith, who lives on the Tarkey House Estate, shouts out, 'I like your new hairstyle, Nell, is it the just got out of bed look?' She smooths her own glossy, chestnut hair with her hand, like the girls on the front of magazines, and sneers at me.

Tanya Noble, her new best friend, is sitting next to her, laughing like it's the funniest joke ever. I don't know what she's got to laugh at with her stupid blue fringe, and bitten fingernails. Craig Boswell kicks his bag into the aisle deliberately, so I stumble, then Kyle Gregson sticks out his foot, tripping me up, as I make my way to my seat.

'Are you all right, Nell?' asks Mr Samuels.

I nod.

'Good, let's get on then. We're studying the life and times of King Charles the Second.'

I spy Michael writing in his special invention note book under the desk. I know that he's working on a fork that will shove food automatically into your mouth, without you having to lift it with your hand, so you can play computer games uninterrupted.

Michael passes me back my jars under the desk. 'I freed 'em,' he says, yawning.

'Thanks,' I say, shoving the jam jars into my rucksack.

I take the screwed-up bit of paper from the zip pocket in my rucksack and smooth it on the desk. I wish I knew what it meant. Michael yawns again.

Sir starts on about some king called Charles and I'm not listening. Instead, I'm studying my ladybirds as they crawl over my desk and the bit of paper that may or may not be a clue.

I read in *Creepy Crawly Fact or Fiction* that when

a ladybird is disturbed, they produce yellow reflex blood, as a warning. This is so cool, I wish I could do that to warn Chantal Smith and Tanya Noble TO KEEP OUT OF MY WAY.

'Nell,' says Mr Samuels.

'Yes, sir,' I say, sitting straight up, shoving the bit of paper quickly in my rucksack.

The whole class turns round and laughs.

'What? What?' I say, looking round. Everyone laughs louder.

'Sir was talking about Nell Gwyn, a lady from history. Not Nell Hobs,' says Michael, with his hand over his eyes. How he manages to pay attention in class and draw his inventions at the same time is beyond my understanding.

'Yes,' says Mr Samuels, 'I was talking about pretty witty Nell, as Samuel Pepys called her in his famous diaries, with her dainty feet.'

I look down at my tiny feet.

'And her curls.'

I shake out my hair.

As for witty, well, I seem to make people laugh whether I want to or not.

'Nell Gwyn was born in Cole Yard Alley, at the top end of Drury Lane in Covent Garden, which was where really poor people lived, and she had to serve drinks in an ale house,' says sir.

My mind flashes back to when I was six, hiding under my bed, shivering with fear when the demon drink first took my mum. But she saw my curls sticking out from under the bed and she laughed and pulled me into the front room to serve beer to all these ugly, sniggering, drunk people, who had been captured by their demon. I wonder if Nell Gwyn ever hid under her bed. No, I bet she was really brave, I reckon Nell Gwyn could've handled herself on the Beckham Estate. I tune my ears back into Mr Samuels' words.

'Nell worked at the Kings Theatre, which is on the very site where the Theatre Royal Drury Lane is today,' says sir.

'My mum takes me to all the shows in that theatre,' shouts out Chantal. 'Next time she says I can bring a friend,' and she puts her arm round Tanya's shoulder and turns round and pulls a face at me.

'Was Nell Gwyn an actress on the stage?' I call out, ignoring her.

'Yes,' says sir, 'but first of all Nell Gwyn worked as an orange-girl for a lady called Orange Moll, who was in charge of all the girls.'

'Sir, what's an orange-girl?' I ask.

'It's what they used to call usherettes in those days because they sold oranges, not half-melted tubs of ice cream,' says sir with a laugh. 'Nell Gwyn, well, she had a big personality and everyone noticed her when she was selling her oranges and she came to the notice of Charles Hart, an actor in the theatre where she worked, who trained her for the stage. At only fourteen years old, she performed at the Kings Theatre.'

'Was she famous, sir?' asks Craig Boswell.

'Yes, Nell Gwyn was really talented and she rose to became a famous comic actress. She was known for dancing a jig at the end of plays. She captured the hearts of the people, and the king fell in love with her.'

And as I listen I know she has captured my heart too.

Chantal Smith's still smirking at me.

I remember watching that TV programme *Who Do You Think You Are*, which traces famous people's ancestors, and that actor from *EastEnders*, Danny Dyer, found out he was related to King Richard III – so why shouldn't I be related to Nell Gwyn? And before I can stop myself, my private daydream comes bursting out.

'Well, for your information,' I say out loud, 'I reckon Nell Gwyn's my ancestor.'

The whole class apart from Michael start laughing again.

'Well, she could be,' I say, 'seeing as how I have tiny feet, curly hair and seem to be able to make you all laugh and most importantly, I AM CALLED NELL!'

My class laugh louder, shrieking, bellowing laughs.

Sir holds his hands up; it's like he's woven a spell and everyone goes quiet.

'I think, Nell Hobs, as you share a name, you should make Nell Gwyn your honorary ancestor.'

'What's that, sir?' I ask.

'Well, it's someone from history who you admire and who becomes a role model, or a guide to how you live your own life. Nell Gwyn was warm-hearted and generous and talented, so there's a lot to admire,' says sir.

'Yeah, Nell Gwyn's my honorary ancestor,' I say, giving my *don't mess with me* look to my whole class.

When you have a mum like mine, you need extra

people in your life; it makes you feel safer, even if they're dead ones from hundreds of years ago.

5

My ladybirds fly away as Mr Samuels draws me into his magical world of the past. I listen hard, because I want to learn about my new honorary ancestor, Nell Gwyn, and the times she lived in. He tells us that King Charles II even remembered Nell Gwyn on his death bed, saying, 'Let not poor Nelly starve.' Sir just makes the history class come alive.

And it's then that Mr Samuels says it. 'Nell Gwyn's mother was an alcoholic.'

My blood freezes. 'Who was her dad, sir?' I blurt out.

'I don't think Nell Gwyn knew him, though some history books say he was a captain, some say a fruitier at Covent Garden.'

It's at that moment that I realise with every breath in my body that my very soul is tied to Nell Gwyn.

I just know she's looking down on me, through the years, and that she understands exactly what it feels like to be me. Nell Gwyn and Nell Hobs. Nell Hobs and Nell Gwyn. Nell and Nell.

I catch a glimmer of gold silk out of the corner of my eye. I turn and look and there she is, Nell Gwyn, and she reaches out her hand to me and she has gone.

'Are you feeling all right, Nell?' asks sir, and I realise my face's frozen.

'Sir, tell us more about that king that liked to go to the theatre.' Michael jumps in to distract Mr Samuels' attention away from me.

'King Charles II loved the theatre and he loved to talk to his subjects,' says Mr Samuels. 'He would stroll around the parks.'

And I know that he lived hundreds of years ago but I just can't help it, this daydream as real as anything comes into my head of King Charles II, having a little strut round the Beckham Estate.

'My beautiful little Nell,' he says, and he bans my mum from ever having a drink again, and he bans the Beckham Street Boyz from hanging round on street corners scaring people, and he makes Michael a knight for his brilliant inventions, and he

gives Aunty Lou lots of gold coins for her kindness and, and—

'Listen to sir,' says Michael, digging me hard in the ribs. A miracle's occurred, Michael's stopped drawing in his invention book and is sitting up like a proper swot.

Sir shows us this portrait of King Charles II. I look at it and drink in his silver tunic with ruffles round the cuffs, and his white tights and silver buckled shoes, and he has this red silken scarf wound around him for decoration, and a cloak of deepest, darkest purple, and he's standing there, looking so kingly, with his long black curly hair.

'Didn't they have no hair straighteners in them days?' says Chantal Smith, flicking back her glistening, straight, chestnut hair.

Mr Samuels just gives her this toe-curling look that makes me have to swallow a giggle.

'It's a wig, Chantal,' he says, 'and was considered to be the height of fashion in the 1600s.'

'I think King Charles' clothes are awesome. I wish that I could wear clothes like that,' says Michael.

Mr Samuels' eyes are twinkling at Michael's words, and the whole class are smirking, but Michael doesn't care, 'cause a smirk is a friend to him compared to what he used to put up with.

Michael was bullied when he first came to live with Aunty Lou. He had a collection of bow ties and a silver jacket and lots of waistcoats and bright-coloured stripy shirts. TJ canerowed Michael's hair and bought him hoodies and trainers to blend in more, but he still got pushed around, 'cause no matter what you look like on the outside if you're a unique and interesting human being on the inside, like Michael – it's going to come shining through.

Then one day, in Mrs Hubert's maths class, he fixed the clock with a remote control device, so that every time she wasn't looking he made the hands on the clock speed forward. Mrs Hubert kept looking at the clock and rubbing her eyes, but she fell for it and we got out of maths forty-five minutes early!

When Mrs Hubert worked out what had happened, Michael got detention for a month but from that moment he was a legend with both the Beckham Street Boyz and the T Crew. They call him Prof M, short for Professor Michael, and he's had no bother since then.

'Yeah, Professor Michael, king of Beckham Estate,' shouts Kyal.

My whole class start drumming their hands on the desk and chanting, 'PROF M, PROF M, PROF M, PROF M, PROF M, PROF M, PROF M.'

'Today,' says Mr Samuels, very calmly and stopping the chants in the wink of a second, 'King Charles is considered to be quite handsome but when he had a portrait painted by Sir Peter Lely and he looked upon it afterwards he asked, "Is that like me? Then odds fish I am an ugly fellow."'

'Odds fish?' Michael laughs.

'Yes, it was his favourite expression,' says Mr Samuels.

But Michael can't stop laughing and saying, 'Odds fish, odds fish,' like a parrot, till the whole class are laughing too.

'I'm going to take you back in time,' says Mr Samuels, casting his spell over me and my whole class. The laughter stops, everyone holds their breath waiting for his next words. 'Back to a time when King Charles II was young, before he went to the theatre and saw Nell Gwyn acting on the stage. His father King Charles I was on the throne and England was a country divided between Roundheads, who followed Oliver Cromwell, and Cavaliers, who followed the king.'

The sun comes out from behind a cloud and shines through the window, sending beams dancing round the class.

'I think we need some fresh air,' says Mr Samuels. 'Can I trust you lot to not disrupt the whole school? I'll meet you by the old girls' changing room in ten minutes.'

And you know what? None of us mess around, not even a little bit, as we make our way outside. Sir must be some sort of miracle worker.

'Greetings,' says Mr Samuels, as he steps out from behind a tree, wearing a long, black, curly wig and a big brimmed hat with a feather, a red tunic with a lacy collar and cuffs and brown leather boots with a turn-over cuff.

Lots of my class take out their phones and start taking photos of him.

But I just drink the clothes in with my eyes, 'cause Mr Samuels looks brilliant.

'No time for that,' says Mr Samuels and he drags out a huge bag filled with helmets and more big brimmed hats with feathers.

'Imagine,' he says, 'the whole of England is split in two. You are either a Cavalier or a Roundhead. The Caviliers were on the side of the king and dressed like me, and the Roundheads followed Oliver Cromwell.'

'Sir, can we try those hats on?' I ask.

'Of course,' says Mr Samuels as he plonks a round helmet on Kyle's head and another on Craig Boswell's. 'The Roundheads wore helmets like these, which gave them their name. However, the Cavalier foot soldiers also wore these helmets, which could make things really confusing during the battles, as to who was fighting on which side.'

'How did they tell each other apart?' asks Michael.

'Well, they wore sashes. The king's army, the Cavaliers or Royalists, wore red sashes, and the Roundheads yellow or tawny orange sashes,' says Mr Samuels.

Yellow sashes! Yellow is the gang colour of the T Crew, from the Tarkey House Estate. They wear yellow bandanas and sir don't even know it. Mr Samuels looks like there is a light inside him as he talks about the olden days.

Mr Samuels splits the class in two. Me and Michael are Cavaliers. Only, whenever sir isn't looking, people keep swapping groups, till everyone on the Beckham Estate is a Cavalier and everyone from Tarkey House is a Roundhead. Oh my days! This is war.

I grab a red hat with a feather on it.

'Sir,' strops Chantal Smith. 'It's not fair. No one will swap with me. I want to be a Cavalier.'

Ha ha, she looks proper minging in her Roundhead helmet.

Mr Richardson, the head teacher, comes round the corner.

'Mr Samuels, you're doing a bit of reenactment I see, splendid!'

Then he sees me. 'Ah, Nell, I understand you were late today.'

My cheeks burn up. I glimpse a spiteful smile on Chantal's face.

'Sorry, sir,' I say. 'I . . .'

Mr Richardson gives me this look like he wants to say something else but then doesn't.

'Nell's been working really hard in my lesson, if I may say so,' says Mr Samuels.

'Good, that's what I like to hear. Umm, Mr Samuels, if I may have a word?'

And they go into a huddle in the corner and none of us dare move or even speak while Mr Richardson's so close. As for me, I daren't even breathe, 'cause

I'm doing what I always do when I see teachers whispering – panicking that it's about me, that a teacher's guessed about Mum's demon. My spine tingles and I want to stand on my head so badly.

At last Mr Richardson walks back towards the school.

'Gather around, everyone,' calls Mr Samuels. 'I have some exciting news.'

I breathe again. Whatever it is it isn't about me.

'The mayor, Felicity Cordour, has declared that this year's Celebrate Heritage Day will be on the life and times of King Charles II. As always it will be on the last day of the summer term. Schools and local businesses will be closed for the afternoon, so that the community can come together.'

Everyone cheers, Michael loudest of all.

I remember the torn newspaper article flapping in the breeze on my way to school. That must have been what it was about.

Mr Samuels takes his hat off with a flourish and bows to us. 'This class has been chosen by Mr Richardson to perform a costume parade, a pageant to celebrate the events of King Charles II's reign. It will take place on the wasteland by the Beckham Estate, finishing by the old youth club.'

Excitement, like a bird's wing fluttering, fills my heart.

'Sir, please can I be Nell Gwyn?' I blurt out. Everyone turns to look at me. 'She's my honorary ancestor, so I should play her. I'd be good at being her, she's my most favourite person in history.'

Nell Gwyn whispers in my ear, 'I am glad you have bagged my role, 'tis yours by rights.'

Mr Samuels smiles his faded smile.

'Nell Hobs, you'll be a perfect Nell Gwyn. We'll have you at the front of the parade, in front of the king, handing out oranges to the crowds.'

'But I want to be Nell Gwyn,' says Chantal, pushing in front of me and stamping on my foot.

'Chantal, as you heard I have just given the part to Nell Hobs – there're lots of other parts you can play. You could be one of the king's serving maids.'

Truly, I think Chantal's going to explode. I have to bite my lip hard and pinch my nose so a snort and a giggle don't escape.

Nell Gwyn chuckles.

'I bet you won't even be able to get a costume,' hisses Chantal in my ear as she strops off, pushing past me to reach Tanya.

Her words punch my belly. She's right. Where

am I going to get a Nell Gwyn costume from? I'll have to try to make one, but with what?

'It's going to be a big occasion,' says Mr Samuels. 'Journalists from *North West London Tonight* will be there to take photographs.'

My mind ticks . . . maybe if I can get my picture in the paper, my dad might see me and claim me. Maybe I look like him and he'll recognise me, 'cause I certainly don't look like my mum.

'Are you going to be in the costume pageant, sir?' asks Michael.

'No, I belong to a reenactment society,' he says. 'We meet and act out the battles from the Civil War. We're going to do a reenactment of the Battle of Naseby, as part of the mayor's festivities.'

'Who won, sir?' shouts Craig.

'The Roundheads, the new model army commanded by Sir Thomas Fairfax and Oliver Cromwell,' says Mr Samuels.

All of the kids from Tarkey House cheer and all of us from the Beckham Estate look like our world's ended.

Sir just has this way of making you care about the people from the past.

I shiver. It feels as if I'm being watched.

I turn round. Chantal Smith is giving me eye daggers and whispering to Tanya.

Then the bell rings, we give our hats and helmets back to sir, but the battle of Roundheads and Cavaliers continues long into break, till there are four Cavaliers and three Roundheads standing outside Mr Richardson's office.

6

At the end of the day, I'm walking home alone, under the gathering dark storm clouds, through the Beckham Estate.

I'm not looking where I'm going and I walk smack into Zak, Bob and Obo, workmen who are sorting out our estate. They've been here so long all us kids have got to know their names.

'Watch where you're going, my girly,' says Obo, as the pile of papers he's carrying go flying everywhere. As he bends down to pick them up, a black curl escapes from his green woollen hat. One of the papers escapes his grasp and flutters off in the wind.

I chase it. I reach and it misses my snatching fingers by a millimetre, and flutters off like a butterfly, and then it lands in a drain.

I pounce on it and scoop it up and, as I look at it

a shiver runs through me. The handwriting on the form is the same as on the smudged scrap of paper in my rucksack. I'm sure of it. I scrabble in my rucksack for the note to compare. Yes, definitely the same. He left a written note with a kiss and a promise to my mum in my flat, number six Beckham Estate.

My heart beats faster and right through me, like a drum.

'Thanks, Nell,' Obo says, taking the form from me.

I follow him as he walks towards his van.

'Obo, do you know my mum?'

'Yes, Nell, everyone knows your mum.'

'Did you write this?' I say shoving the note in his face.

'I might've done.'

'It's got a kiss on it. I found it in my flat.'

'Nell,' he says, laughing, 'go home and do your homework, or whatever you have to do.' He climbs in the driver's seat and slams the door. I wave him goodbye as he drives off.

Do your homework! That seems a very dad-like thing to say. Definitely a possible candidate for the position of my father.

As my thoughts are whirring, there's a loud beep. I leap out of the way of a Rentokil van that veers past me. A bald man shakes his fist at me. I catch my breath as I watch it make its bumpy way, over the wasteland, towards the old youth club. I turn back on my heel and walk towards the flats and I very nearly step on a giant Oriental cockroach that's making a hasty exit. I must help it escape from the angry Rentokil man. That would not be a nice fate for the cockroach.

I whip out a jam jar from my khaki rucksack and let the cockroach crawl in. Its long antennae wave around.

Cockroaches, well, they can eat anything, so I rip a page out of my maths book for him to much on. Cockroaches could survive nuclear war but I bet they wouldn't survive Mrs Hubert's boring maths lessons.

A pair of black ballet shoes come into my vision.

'Nell, what you got there?'

I straighten up coming face to face with Sasha, who lives on the eleventh floor of the Beckham Estate.

I hold out the jar so she can see it, my cheeks on fire, no words come.

'That's proper enormous,' she says, laughing as she flicks her long black hair away from her face. Sasha's so pretty and really good at singing. She goes to Performing Arts college so she can actually learn to be an actress like Nell Gwyn.

Her dad, Fox, was a really famous rock star in this band called Zebra Blue, and now he runs the Archie Dobbs Music Project in the space under our flats.

Sasha's trainers are slung over her shoulder the laces in a bow.

'They're new,' she says, 'and they're proper pinching my toes. Walk with me Nell.' We make our way back towards the flats and Sasha tells me all about her acting classes. I just listen in wonder, too shy and impressed to talk.

I can see Bernie from Bernie's Burger Bar sweeping the pavement outside his shop.

'All right my diamond girls?' he calls.

'All right Bernie,' shouts Sasha.

I smile and wave.

We reach the Archie Dobbs Music Project and I can hear someone playing the guitar and a dog howling. It's Buster, Finn's dog. As a naturalist I'm good at recognising the different Staffie barks.

There are a lot of Staffordshire Bull Terriers on our estate, so this is a useful skill to have.

'That's Finn playing,' says Sasha. 'I'd know that racket anywhere. Nell I'm going to go quick, before he sees me and I end up distracted and spend the whole evening with him. I've got loads of homework,' and she gives me a hug, before running towards the lift.

I go down the slope and into the music project room. Finn winks at me. 'All right Nell,' he says over the music. Buster's stopped howling and is chewing a drumstick.

'WOULD YOU LIKE ME TO TAKE BUSTER BACK TO YOUR FLAT SO YOU CAN PRACTISE YOUR GUITAR, FINN?' I shout.

He shakes his head as the electric guitar makes a *whar whar* sound, so loud it hurts my ears.

'BUT I DON'T MIND, HONEST. WOULDN'T IT BE HELPFUL TO YOU?'

Finn ignores me and carries on playing, so I balance the jam jar with my cockroach specimen on a drum, so I can stand on my head with my feet against one of the pillars holding our flats up.

I love looking at all the upside-down drums and guitars and saxophones and trumpets as the blood rushes to my brain. Finn's guitar playing sounds better upside down too.

Finn puts down the guitar, sits on a box and stares at me.

I can't stand on my head a second longer, so I turn the right way up and stare right back at him.

'Don't you want to go home, Nell?'

And all the thoughts of if Obo might be my dad just vanish and the truth fills me up, 'cause I *don't* want to go home. I'm too scared of what I might find.

I shake my head, swallowing. No way am I going to cry in front of Finn.

'Here,' he says and pulls out a Snickers bar from his pocket. 'Go on, take it.'

And before I can help myself, I have ripped off the paper and crammed the bar in my mouth, like a piglet, 'cause I have had no breakfast and no lunch.

Finn turns his head quickly away and starts rummaging in his pocket again.

His voice has this crack in it as he shoves another Snickers bar in my hand.

'Here we go, have this one as well.'

And I take it and put it in my rucksack, because Mum might not be up to making tea tonight and it's always good to have emergency supplies.

Last week, I ended up eating the raw carrots Aunty Lou gave me for Asbo and Chaos. I hated myself, because a naturalist should not deprive animals of food. Aunty Lou would've gone mad if she'd known, and would have had me round at her flat in a jiffy but I can't go running to her for every little thing.

I grab the jam jar and push through the Zebra Blue Community Choir, who are coming into the Music Project to practise, and then I drag my feet slowly, all the way to my flat.

Before I even ring the bell the door opens, and there's Mum, in jeans and her favourite yellow top. She's kept her *pinkie promise* to me. Hair brushed, eyes sparkling with just a touch of redness. She smells of honeysuckle perfume and is as clean and fresh as the morning dew. Her pretty rosebud mouth is set in a chirpy smile.

'My darling Nell,' she says, like a mum from a TV advert, and pulls me into the flat by my elbow.

The table is laden with the most scrumptious tea ever.

Everything's on sticks: mini burgers, a bowl of hot chips, mini tomatoes. Then there are fairy cakes and mini chocolate eclairs and a bowl of

Quality Street, with the wrappers taken off, each one with a stick through it. No word of a lie, this is like Mum's perfect tea, little things to nibble at 'cause her demon steals her appetite. I'll have to make sure she eats.

Mum laughs and claps her hands. There are bottles of Coke and lemonade in the middle of the table, no wine or beer or anything. I breathe a sigh of relief.

'See, my darling Nelly nell nell. We can dance and sing and eat at the same time. Like a party. No need to bother with dull knives and forks. See how much I love you.'

'Thanks, Mum,' I say, my smile nearly cracking my face open, 'but I got to go next door to feed my animal family before we eat.'

'No need.' And she pulls me into my bedroom by my elbow and there are all my animals, fed and cleaned and watered.

Beyoncé and Destiny are swimming round and round in a sparkling clean bowl. Asbo and Chaos are chomping on celery sticks, Bob Marley is chilling and chewing on dandelions and Fiz and Tyrone's gerbilarium have been cleaned out, and they're busy tucking into their gerbil food. Aunty Lou hamster is going round and round in her wheel, in her lovely clean cage.

Mum's looking at me like a little girl who wants to please *her* mum. It should be the other way round.

'Have I done it right?' she asks.

'You've fed my animal family perfectly,' I say, 'thank you.'

'Goodness, what have you got there?' she asks, peering into my jam jar.

'An oriental cockroach,' I say.

I can see Mum's trying her best not to shudder as she takes the jam jar from me and puts it on the windowsill.

'You didn't get your love of creepy crawlies from me.'

'Did my dad like bugs?' I ask before I can stop myself, because I don't want to ruin her mood. I hold my breath but she acts like I haven't spoken.

'Let's get you out of that school uniform, I do so hate dull clothes.'

She takes my favourite jeans and sparkly butterfly T-shirt from my wardrobe and stands in front of my bedside table while I get changed.

'You won't leave me, Mum, will you? You'll stay in with me all evening.'

'Course I will, don't be silly.'

And I hug her, and gradually her hug becomes stronger and I feel safe with her for the first time in what seems like for ever.

Then Mum takes my hand and pulls me back into the kitchen and puts on that Beyoncé song about single ladies. Beyoncé is Mum's favourite, she even went to see her in concert once.

I load a plate of things on sticks for each of us, and my anxieties vanish as my hungry mouth bites into the scrummy food. I see Mum tuck into her mini burgers and chips, and when our bellies are full, I move behind Mum, both of us waggling one hand in the air, like Beyoncé. We dance and sing and we sparkle all evening.

Finally, we flop down on the sofa.

'This is the perfect party for two,' says Mum.

'Mum,' I ask, 'when you used to go to parties before I was born, were they around here?'

'Yes, Camden was always buzzing, and most of my friends were local. Why do you ask?'

'No reason, just interested, that's all.' But inside I'm thinking, it stands to reason then that my dad's from this area.

I take a deep breath. 'Mum.'

'Yeah?'

'Obo, the workman who wears that green woolly hat, says he knows you.'

'Yeah, of course I know Obo,' says Mum and then she switches the telly on and I daren't ask her any more in case it spoils the evening.

We watch Lucy Cook's animal programme and then I get Fiz and Tyrone from their gerbilarium and we let the little gerbils run over our hands as we watch *Coronation Street*. It's the best time ever. When it's over I put them back in their gerbilarium, as Mum switches off the TV.

'Come and tell me about school,' she says, patting the cushion next to her.

We snuggle on the sofa as I tell Mum about pretty witty Nell Gwyn, with her dainty feet and curly hair, and how she acted and danced for the king and he loved her with all his heart.

'She's my honorary ancestor and I think that's why you called me Nell, even though you'd didn't know it at the time.'

'Well,' says Mum, winking at me, 'I bet it *was* why I called you Nell, with your dainty feet and pretty curly hair.'

'And guess what, Mum? I'm going to be Nell

Gwyn in the pageant, but I'll need a costume.'

Mum jumps up and runs into her bedroom. I can hear the sound of dragging and of lots of things been thrown around.

Eventually, Mum comes running back in, carrying a bundle of faded gold material. It's beautiful, with little beads embroidered on it.

'I was a bridesmaid, before you were born. The dress got ruined, but my nan bought too much material when she made it.'

'So you'll help me make a Nell Gwyn costume?'

'Course I will.' And we link our little fingers.

'*Pinkie promise.*'

'*Pinkie promise.*'

I hug my mum and I'm as happy as happy can be.

I wrap the material around me, and twirl round, pretending I'm dancing on the stage in the theatre, for the king, but as I point my feet and swirl and jig around, Mum's feet start jigging too, and her hands start shaking, which always happens when she needs a drink, so I start to dance harder.

'Look at me, Mum, please look at me.' But she keeps sighing and biting her lip and glancing at the door.

'Look at me, Mum.' I dance faster. 'I'm Nell

Gwyn.' But Mum gets up and runs out of the door.

Our perfect, sparkly evening vanishes. I hear the front door bang and the lock turn and then she's gone.

7

I scramble on to the draining board and wriggle out of the window.

The sky's belly rumbles with anger and a thunder clap explodes. Sheets of raindrops sting my face.

'Mum,' I call, 'Mum!'

A flash of lightning shoots from the sky and I see her, right across the courtyard, running towards Mr and Mrs Patel's newsagents. I run after her and as I reach the shop, I kneel on the cold, wet pavement and peep through the bottom of the door. If the Patels see me they'll make me go home, and Mrs Patel might want to come with me and I just want my mum. I need to stick with Mum and make sure she's safe.

Mrs Patel has her hand on Mum's arm.

'Please, Stacey, go home. You should be looking after Nell.'

'Fine, keep your drink. I'll find it somewhere else!'

Mum shakes Mrs Patel's arm off, and her rosebud mouth turns into a snarl of ripped petals.

'My money's as good as anyone's. All I want is one little drink.' She's shaking.

Mr Patel comes out of the stock room.

'Stacey, we will not serve you. Go to your child.'

Mum bolts back through the door of the shop and I roll out of the way just in time. I jump up and run after her. I reach out and grab her arm.

'Mum, please, I want to finish dancing for you.'

'Nell, go home!' Mum turns round and her face is all twisted and ugly like a monster. The demon has won, stretching its claws out towards me. She doesn't look like my mum and she disappears into the dark night.

'Mum!' I scream after her. 'You *PINKIE PROMISED* you would help me make my costume!'

Raindrops sting my eyes and trickle down my back.

I suddenly need to see my animal family, so I go home.

As I switch on my bedroom light the empty bedside table hits me. My Noah's ark charm bracelet's gone. Then I remember Mum standing in front of my bedside table, when I was getting changed. She must've taken it down to Percy's Pawnbrokers in Kentish Town, to get money. Mum's sold my birthday present.

A knock at the door. My bones jolt. Supposing it's the police or someone coming to tell me that Mum's hurt. I climb up on to the draining board, push open the kitchen window and poke my head out. It's TJ, standing in the now gentle rain, carrying some planks of wood.

'Just checking up on you, Nell,' he says, walking to the window. 'Where's your mum?'

'She's asleep,' my whispers lie. 'Shhhh. I don't want to wake her. TJ, you'd best go, you're going to get soaked.'

'It's only drizzling,' he says. 'Look, Nell, I stopped off on the way home from college to pick this up.' He nods to the planks of wood in his hand.

'What for?' I ask.

'You'll see,' he says, winking.

There's a pause as his eyes look at me, searching for something.

'You sure you don't want to stop at ours tonight?' he asks.

'I'm sure,' I say. I hate lying to TJ but I've got to wait for Mum, see she's safe.

'I'll text Mum,' says TJ, 'tell her you're OK.'

He puts his hand in his pocket, pulls out three pound coins and hands them through the window.

'Here, have this for your animal food fund and say hello to your little tortoise man from me.'

'Thanks, TJ,' I say, taking the money. 'I'd better go, I don't want to wake Mum.' I close the window.

I'm just putting the coins in my *Ark Fund* jar in my bedroom when the lights go out. My coins jingle in the dark. No electricity. Mum's not put any money on the meter key again!

'Don't be scared,' I say to my animal family, being careful not to show in my voice that I feel scared myself, 'cause animals pick up on these things. 'It'll soon be morning,' I say.

I feel my way back into the kitchen. I wish I could see in the dark like a bat can. I open the bits and bobs drawer and grope for the torch. A naturalist should always have a torch. The light shines on the gold material, which has fallen on the kitchen floor.

Wrapping it round me, I go back to my bedroom, kick off my wet clothes, pull on my PJs and curl up on my bed. I'm too tired to even stand on my head.

My eyes start to droop but I must keep awake to wait for Mum . . .

Nell Gwyn gives me a saucy wink as she acts her part to the audience. Laughter explodes around me. Then she starts to do a jig, pointing her pretty, pretty feet, whirling around the stage so quickly her toes are a blur. I am sitting in the front row of the Kings Theatre on a green bench in my purple dressing gown.

The sun shines down on me from the blue sky above and all around me orange-girls cry, 'Oranges, come buy my sweet oranges.'

The smell from the oranges and the hot wax from the candles that light the stage fill my nostrils. There is chatting all around me as gentlemen dressed in fine breeches, gloves, tunics and hats with big brims and plumes of feathers call to each other, and the ladies dressed in the most beautiful silken gowns of silvers, purples, turquoises and indigos I have ever seen peep from behind masks.

Nell, in her golden gown, beckons me on to the stage and takes my hand, and we dance for the king, who blows a kiss to Nell, and smiles and waves to me.

I wake with a jolt.

I go into Mum's bedroom; by the torchlight I can see her bed's empty. My heart hits the carpet. She still isn't home. Her bedside clock says three o'clock in the morning.

I use my torch to do a night-time animal check. Bob Marley's tucked inside his shell. It must be nice being a tortoise, able to hide inside a shell when the outside world gets too scary. I crawl under the covers, praying Mum'll be home in the morning.

8

Next morning, I find Mum slumped over on the kitchen table again.

I check she's breathing, put a glass of water and headache tablets by her hand and the sick bowl next to her.

And then I deliberately bang around the kitchen. I grab one of the leftover mini burgers for breakfast but it's cold and tastes greasy.

Despite Mum acting like a TV advert mum for nearly one whole evening, none of the laundry's been done. I have to put on my dirty uniform again. I shove the jam jar holding the cockroach into my rucksack, jump on to the draining board and wriggle out of the window.

I find a lump of lovely moss round the back of the flats. I release my cockroach on to it, so he'll be safe. He's made good work of munching through the page of my maths book.

Mrs Patel's in the doorway of her shop.

'There you are, Nell. I have been looking out for you. Come quick.' She takes my hand and pulls me behind the counter. 'Something for you to take to school.'

She has made me a packed lunch!

'Thank you, Mrs Patel,' I say, a sparkler of light breaking through my sadness cloud.

She hands me the latest copy of *Creepy Crawly Fact or Fiction*. It has a colony of ants on the front.

'Has Mum paid my bill?'

'Never you mind, it's my little treat.'

I give her a hug.

I contemplate the Dad issue. If I had a dad, he could pay Mum's paper bill, he would give me a packed lunch and a lift to school and and . . .

Bernie from Bernie's Burger Bar is wiping down the tables. He calls and gives me a wave.

'You be a good girl at school today, do you hear me?'

By the time I reach school, lessons have started. I'm meant to be in maths but I duck into the library and head for the history section. I find a book called *Costume Through History*.

Mrs Maple, the librarian, is putting books on a shelf from her trolley. She hasn't seen me yet, so I flop down on a red bean bag and start to flick through the book, sneaking a cheeky peek at my packed lunch. Lovely cheese and tomato sandwiches, with crispy lettuce and pickle. A tangerine and a KitKat and a carton of apple juice. I bite into the KitKat 'cause I'm starving.

Mrs Maple looks up and smiles when she sees me.

'Shouldn't you be in class, Nell?' She tugs at her comfy-looking blue sweater.

'I know I'm late, but I really need to take this book out, please?'

'OK, give it to me.' She takes the book over to her desk, stamps it and hands it back to me.

I open it immediately and turn the pages through all the olden times, back to the 1950s, 1940s, back and back and back to the Victorian times, and then back some more. I reach Charles II and my heart stops. There she is smiling up at me. It's a picture of Nell Gwyn, in a golden dress, just like in my dreams. The silky dress falls in glistening folds, with a white collar and cuffs. And her arm's draped round a lamb, which is nuzzling into her hand. Nell Gwyn must have been a naturalist too. Nell has an almost smile on her face.

'Get to class, Nell. NOW,' says Mrs Maple.

I continue to read my book as I walk down the corridor.

Thud!

My bottom hits the floor and my book flies straight out of my hand. Chantal Smith is standing over me.

'Well, if it isn't Smelly Nelly. Look at the state of you. Hasn't your mum got an iron? Haven't you got a comb?'

My costume book is lying in the middle of the corridor on the Nell Gwyn page. I scramble up and run to grab it but Chantal gets there first.

'What's this? Oh, for your costume, is it? Is it going to come from a jumble sale?'

'GIVE ME MY BOOK BACK!' I shout.

Mr Richardson comes storming out of his office.

'What is this shouting? Why are you girls out of your class? This is unacceptable behaviour!'

'Mrs Hubert asked me to go to the office, to say that our whiteboard isn't working. Nell's only just got into school, sir, and by accident we bumped into each other. I was trying to help her and give her book back to her but she started shouting at me.'

Chantal shoves the book in my hand.

'Nell, why are you late?'

I open my mouth and shut it like Beyoncé and Destiny do, but no words come.

'WELL?' shouts Mr Richardson.

Then I'm saved. Click-clacking on her heels down the corridor comes Miss Petunia, my biology teacher, her red ponytail swinging as she walks, crisp and pretty in a green dress.

'Mr Richardson, as Nell's late for school, I wondered if she could help me tidy the biology lab. Year ten left it in a terrible mess. I have a free period and I need to get it ready for my next lesson.' Her eyes sparkle at me, while her mouth pretends to be stern.

'Certainly, Miss Petunia, that sounds like a very fitting punishment, and Nell, remember when you've completed your punishment, you must sign in my punishment book.'

'Yes, Mr Richardson,' I say. 'Sorry for being late, Mr Richardson.'

And my heart dances, 'cause that isn't a punishment at all. I run ahead of Miss Petunia to reach my favourite room in the whole school. I fling my costume book and school rucksack down and whirl around, past Fred the skeleton, and past the pictures of bugs and animals from all over the world.

Miss Petunia stands in the doorway watching me. I stop spinning by the display of photographs of my fox rescue that I made for Miss Petunia's wall. She smiles at me and I don't know if it's her smile of kindness, or because I feel safe in the biology lab, but all the happenings of yesterday evening fill me up and hot tears bounce down my cheeks, and I swallow but I can't stop them so I stand on my head, right in the middle of the biology lab.

'Nell, would you come the right way up, please? I need to talk to you.'

I flop on to the floor. Miss Petunia beckons me to a chair next to her.

'What's wrong?' she says.

I shake my head and swallow again. 'Nothing, miss.'

Miss Petunia looks at me for the longest time and then she says, 'Nell, I have a secret to tell you. You mustn't tell anyone but at parents' evening you're going to be awarded the Borough Nature Prize by Mayor Felicity Cordour, for your fox rescue and for your outstanding work in biology.'

My jaw drops and I do a goldfish impression for

the second time that morning, because I have never won a prize before in my whole life.

I nearly hug Miss Petunia but then I remember you don't hug teachers.

Miss Petunia laughs. 'I thought that would put a spring back in your step,' she says. 'Remember it's a secret at the moment but I thought I should tell you as you look so sad.'

I stay and help Miss Petunia, and as I fold white coats, straighten jars, dust Fred the skeleton and push the Blu-Tack on my fox display more firmly into the wall, my higgledy-piggledy thoughts start to take order in my head. I have the pageant to look forward to and now I've won the Borough Nature Prize! I know that Mum will be prouder than the whole universe when she comes to parents' evening. So proud, maybe, that she will find the strength not to drink. Hope starts to trickle into my heart.

'A *North West London Tonight* photographer will be at prize-giving,' says Miss Petunia. 'So you'll have your photograph in the paper for rescuing the fox.'

So that's two chances to be in the paper: the pageant and prize-giving. A newspaper that goes all over this part of London. Surely there's a chance my dad'll see it. I am sure any dad would love a daughter who has won the Borough Nature Prize. The bell rings for break.

'Thanks, Miss Petunia, no word of a lie, this is the best news ever.' I snatch up my rucksack and run out of the lab.

I find Michael sitting alone on a bench just staring up at the sky.

I long to tell him about my prize, but I hug my secret close to me.

'Odds fish,' I say, plonking myself next to him.

'Odds fish,' he says but he looks sad. 'I like looking up at the clouds,' he says, 'it makes me feel good that at least Mum and me are both under the same sky, even if she is in Jamaica.'

'Was it OK?' I ask. 'Seeing your dad?'

Michael shrugs his shoulders. 'We just stood there looking at each other, no words came for the longest time.'

'At least you've got a dad,' I say. I bury into my rucksack and bring out the clue.

'Michael, I think Obo might be my dad. Look at this, it's to my mum and it's got a kiss on it.'

'But, Nell, lots of people put kisses—'

'And he called me his girly and he told me to do my homework.'

Michael gives me a funny look.

'Michael, I've got to find my dad, 'cause he can help me with Mum and if he's got his own family, maybe I can stay there sometimes.'

Michael grins. 'Well, I saw Obo chatting to your mum outside Patel's, when he bought a paper. Could be him. Or your dad could be an astronaut.'

'Or a deep-sea diver,' I say.

'Or the tallest man in the world,' says Michael.

'Or the shortest,' I say. 'I just know I got a dad somewhere.'

And we both look up at the clouds.

9

After school, I race out of the school gates alone 'cause Michael's in detention for using the school canteen forks to work on his invention. The kids who have school dinners had to use a knife and spoon.

I'm right at the end of the road when I remember, I forgot to sign Mr Richardson's stupid punishment book!

I race back up the road, through the school gates and all the way to Mr Richardson's office. His door's not closed properly. I peep through the gap to see if he's there.

He's sorting through a pile of photographs in a drawer and laying them out on his desk.

I lift my arm to knock, but my fist freezes in mid-air as Mr Richardson scoops a spider up from his desk in his hand.

'There you are, my beauty,' he says, walking oh

so carefully to the half open window and setting the spider free.

Mr Richardson is a naturalist! I'm seeing him in a whole new light.

He looks up and sees me. 'Ah, Nell, come in, come in, don't just stand there.'

I go in and stand in front of his desk.

'You've just caught me. I was staying behind to sort out some old photos to stick in the album my wife gave me for my birthday.'

'Please, Mr Richardson, sir, I forgot to write in your punishment book.'

And he does this kind of smile as he swivels the book round and hands me a pen. Mr Richardson never ever smiles when people have to write in the punishment book.

The punishment book looks like Michael's diary. All I can see is *Michael*, *Michael*, *Michael*, *Michael*, *Michael*. I write underneath:

Name	Reason for punishment	Teacher supervising	Punishment	What I have learned
Michael Henry	Using forks for invention	Mrs Hubert	Detention	Forks are for eating with
Nell Hobs	I was late again	Miss Petunia	Tidying lab	Be on time for school

'Thank you, Mr Richardson, sorry for being late, Mr Richardson.' I go to hand him back his pen.

'Is everything all right, Nell? You look very tired. Maybe I should call your mum in for a coffee and a little chat. You've been late for school a lot.'

I drop the pen; it rolls across the blue carpet.

A coffee and a chat with Mum! My mind whizzes round. Mum would probably not turn up, or would smell of drink and then what would happen? Mr Richardson could report her and I could get sent away from my animal family to foster care. I can't leave Mum!

I need to get out of here but as I turn round my rucksack catches the pile of photographs on his desk and they flutter to the floor.

'I'm so sorry, sir,' I say, kneeling down and gathering up his pen and the photos.

On the top of my scooped-up pile's an old photograph showing lots of people climbing into a coach with *Beyoncé concert* written in a banner at the front. A young-looking Mr Richardson is at the front of the crowd, wearing a baseball cap, and then I see her. It's Mum, standing behind Mr Richardson, laughing and looking so pretty, like she used to, before the demon got her. Mum and Mr Richardson went to the same Beyoncé concert and the photograph looks about twelve years old. Could *he* possibly be my dad?

'Mr Richardson, you went to a Beyoncé concert with my mum?'

He takes the photograph and looks at it. 'Oh, yes, I did indeed, we sat next to each other on the coach, as I recall. It was a memorable evening.'

I look at the framed photograph on the wall of Mrs Richardson and the three boy Richardsons with curly, combed, tidy hair, all holding violins under their chins, and I wonder what it would be like if Mr Richardson was my dad. Maybe I'd play the trumpet. I picture Buster and me marching round the Beckham Estate, me blowing my trumpet and Buster howling and people opening their windows and yelling at us to shut up. I try to picture myself standing in the middle of the three boys with violins in the photograph, smiling with combed hair, and I just can't. They all look smug and tidy, like they've never ever had to write their names in the punishment book in their whole lives.

I shudder. Me living with the headmaster? Oh, no, no, no.

'Sorry, Mr Richardson, I've got to go.' I race out of his office.

The playground's deserted. I stand on my head till the images of Mr Richardson being my dad vanish, and my secret happy bubble about winning the nature prize comes back. I see a pair of legs walk towards me and I drop my own legs drop back to the ground and turn the right way up. It's Rulla Miller, the head girl, carrying a pile of books. She shakes her long honey hair.

'Standing on your head to make your troubles vanish?' she says.

I gape at her. She gets it!

She flings her books on the floor and turns a cartwheel.

'That's what I do,' she says, gathers her books up, winks at me and dashes off.

I run all the way home and bang on my front door and shout, 'MUM!' I wait . . . nothing.

So I keep on shouting and banging,

'MUM, MUUUUM,' I shout, but still nothing.

My secret happy bubble about winning the Borough Nature Prize pops, and knives of anger and fear fill me as I worry where Mum is. Supposing she's fallen and is trapped somewhere, hurt and calling for me, and I can't get to her. I open the letter box and peer through. I can hear Asbo and Chaos doing their guinea pig singing. They're hungry.

'It's OK, I'm here,' I call to Beyoncé, Destiny, Bob Marley, Aunty Lou hamster, Fiz and Tyrone and Asbo and Chaos.

It's Friday evening, so Aunty Lou'll be at church, she always helps get it ready for Sunday. I knock to see if TJ's in but there's no answer.

My tummy rumbles. I perch my bottom on the doorstep, and gobble up the last cheese and tomato sandwich from Mrs Patel's packed lunch. It starts to rain again, so I quickly run across the courtyard, towards the newsagent. Obo, Bob and Zak, who have been filling in the cracks in the courtyard, run and take shelter in their van. Obo winds down the window.

'Get out of the rain, Nell,' he shouts.

'I'm just getting something from the shops for my mum,' I lie, shouting back.

Get out of the rain, he'd said! That's definitely the type of thing dads say.

Mrs Patel smiles as I walk into her shop.

'Thank you, Mrs Patel,' I say in my best, most polite voice, 'your lunch was delicious.'

'It is my pleasure, you lovely, lovely girl,' says Mrs Patel, still smiling.

Then her face changes. I hear the bell jangle as the shop door's pushed open. A brown nose pokes through.

'Out now, come on, out, out.'

It's Buster. He runs into the shop, jumps up and gives me a Staffie kiss.

'This is the fourth time today that naughty dog has come into my shop. Look at that, there are muddy, wet paw prints all over my shop floor.'

'Buster just likes exploring, Mrs Patel,' I explain.

Then I see a squashed tennis ball under the shelf, where all the magazines are displayed. I lie flat on my tummy and pull it out.

'Oh, he just wants this back,' I say.

'How did that nasty, dirty ball get in here?'

Buster wags his tail and barks.

Mr Patel appears out of the stock room with a lettuce and some carrots. 'For your zoo, Nell,' he says, chuckling.

'Thanks, Mr Patel,' I say.

The rain outside turns to drizzle.

'Is your mum home?' asks Mrs Patel, putting the lettuce and carrots in a bag.

'Yes,' I lie. 'I'll take Buster.' I grab the ball and the vegetables with one hand and Buster's collar with the other, and hurry out of the shop before they can ask me any more questions.

I run across the courtyard, Buster running in front of me, tripping me up.

Through the window of number one, I see an old lady I haven't seen before, holding a cute black and tan Cavalier King Charles spaniel, and smiling at me. I smile back but she vanishes behind the curtain.

I bang on my front door again, but still nothing. I run with Buster to the lift, then up to the eleventh floor to Finn's flat, where he lives with his mum, Trisha.

As soon as Trisha opens the door, Buster darts through it. I give Trisha the squashed ball.

'Oh, Nell, you angel. I was trying to clean Buster's teeth, like the vet said. Only Buster weren't having it, gave me the slip.'

I need to keep busy, to keep the worry thoughts about Mum away from my heart.

'Can I help you with Buster? I'm a good dog-teeth cleaner.'

'There's someone who you can help,' she says.

I turn to look, and there's the old lady who owns Napoleon, the ginger cat, though mostly, as I've said, he spends his time invading other people's flats.

She's staggering along with four bags of shopping.

I run up to her and take the bags from her.

'Thank you, my duck. My bones are weary. I've bought lots of food for Waffles.'

Waffles? That must be her cat's real name. He doesn't look like a Waffles. I think the name Napoleon that people on the Beckham Estate call him suits him much better.

The bags are heavy, stuffed full with tins of cat food. It's hard carrying them along with my bag of carrots and lettuce and my school rucksack.

I stagger along to her flat where Napoleon's waiting at her front door. He comes and rubs himself against my legs as she forces her key into her front door lock.

'Thanks, duck,' she says again, shutting the door in my face before I can ask her if there are any other jobs she wants doing. She just misses Napoleon's tail as he dives in.

'Now what?' I do pigeon steps back to the smelly lift and ride up to the eighteenth floor and then press the button to go down. I've had to do this lots of times, up and down, up and down, waiting for Mum to come home.

I hear the rain stop as the lift doors open and

there's Mum twirling round, splashing through the puddles in her denim mini skirt and stained white top, trying to get Zak, Bob and Obo to dance with her.

I can't feel my legs, they're all wobbly.

'Come on, boys, it's time for a party, dance with me!' she screeches as she grabs hold of Zak and spins him around, splashing his hot tea everywhere.

'Go home, love,' says a workman with ginger hair and stubble. 'We got work to do.'

'You're all dull, dull, dull. Nell, stop being a boring little kid, come and dance with your mum.'

'No, Mum, please, I want you to come home,' I say, feeling sick as people start to watch.

Mum begins wiggling her bum and singing that Beyoncé song about being crazy in love.

Obo, Zak and Bob just sit there, drinking tea and laughing at her. My blood fizzles. Surely Obo, if he is my dad, should be helping with the situation, not laughing. I look into his eyes, searching, searching for the secrets in his soul. Is he? Could he be my dad? He looks up and meets my gaze and his expression changes. He jumps up, splashing tea down his jeans, and grabs Mum's arm.

'Come on, Stacey, you need to get yourself home.'

Mum flings her arms around him. 'Dance with me, Obo,' and she whirls him around.

Then Mum lets go of Obo and whizzes round with her arms in the air.

'WEEEEEEEEE,' she screeches and falls over showing her knickers.

I want to die right there and then.

'Stacey, you're making a show of yourself. Come on, Nell needs her dinner.' Obo pulls Mum up off the ground.

More people stop to stare; there are people on the lower balconies of the flats laughing. Then shame swallows me whole as Sasha walks towards the lift, hair in a bun, on her way back from college. Oh no, no, no, I don't want her to see my mum like this.

A silent scream rises up through me.

'You're all no fun. Let's have a party!' Mum laughs and starts to dance by herself again. I close my eyes.

I am at the Kings Theatre. Nell Gwyn stands centre stage, acting a funny part, and the audience are laughing and clapping and cheering. The theatre is filled with love, laughter and warmth for Nell Gwyn. She holds out her arms to me. I go up on to the stage and she swirls me round in a dance.

It is beautiful.

I open my eyes. *This* is ugly.

My scream is no longer silent. 'MUM, COME HOME NOW. I NEED TO FEED MY ANIMALS. YOU LOCKED ME OUT.'

Aunty Lou strides across the courtyard, takes one look at the situation and storms up to Mum, fury on her lips.

Sasha runs over and takes one of Mum's arms and Aunty Lou the other and they march her back home. I follow.

Mum has the key in her pocket. Sasha gives my burning cheek a kiss and leaves us. Aunty Lou unlocks the door, takes Mum into her bedroom and starts shouting at her.

Odd words float into the kitchen. 'Neglecting . . . attention . . . love Nell . . . selfish . . .'

Mum's sobbing '. . . sorry . . .'

I run into my bedroom to feed my animals and remember I need more supplies. I must get to the pet shop in Kentish Town before it closes.

I shake my Ark Fund jar . . . but it's empty.

Mum's taken the money. *My* money.

I turn round. Aunty Lou's behind me, watching.

'Oh, child,' she says and takes me in her arms.

'I've only got this,' I say, passing her the plastic bag that Mr and Mrs Patel gave me. Aunty Lou marches into our kitchen and starts chopping up the lettuce and carrots. She likes to chop vegetables when she's vexed. The poor carrots don't stand a chance.

'Give your zoo this, and then we'll get them over to ours. You're not staying here. It's time for *Operation Ark*.'

Only we don't have to climb through the window in the dead of night. Out we march, through the front door, all my animal family, two by two, and finally Bob Marley and me. I can't help it, though I feel so angry – I turn my head towards her shut bedroom door and with a tiny shimmering breath I whisper, 'I love you, Mum.'

10

'Michael, put Chaos on my belly.'

I'm lying on the grass on the wasteland by the side of the old youth club. It's sunny, with a nice breeze; lovely weather for guinea pigs but I'm feeling woozy.

'Why, Nell?' Michael's lying by my side wearing a green shirt with polka dots, an orange bow tie, and his favourite silver jacket.

''Cause in the Andes, in Peru, doctors put guinea pigs on someone when they are feeling unwell and they squeak when they're on the bit of the body that's ill. And I'm feeling really sick this morning.'

'You're mad, Nell,' says Michael, plonking Chaos on top of me.

I do not think the doctors in Peru would've employed Asbo and Chaos as medical assistants 'cause they start running up and down me, squealing with joy at their new game, tickling me with their little claws, till I'm laughing all my Mum worries away. Then they get tangled in my hair and Michael has to rescue them. Bob Marley just chews dandelions and watches.

'Maybe you feel sick 'cause you've had no breakfast,' says Michael, pulling out half a sticky bun from his pocket. I peel off bits of paper bag that are stuck to it and a metal spring from one of Michael's inventions that has wedged in the icing and, as I chew, I do feel a bit better. A naturalist in the wilds must make the most of their provisions, as they do not know how long they'll be out there for.

We lie on our sides and make a human guinea pig pen and we put Bob Marley, Asbo and Chaos inside. Michael and I don't have to use words to communicate. Sometimes no words is nice. We watch Asbo and Chaos running around guinea pig singing, and Bob Marley chomping on clover.

I grab my courage and break the silence.

'Michael, you know Nell Gwyn?'

'Your honorary ancestor?'

'Yes, that's right, well, sometimes I see her and she chats to me and in my dreams I'm with her dancing on the stage for the king.' Michael's staring at me, chewing on a long bit of grass. 'You do believe me, don't you? I'm not making it up, honest.'

Michael nods. 'Yeah, I do. Sometimes I have chats to Leonardo da Vinci in my head and in my dreams. He's very interested in my inventions. He says I am a man ahead of my time, like him. Do you know he invented the helicopter 450 years ahead of us using them?'

'No word of a lie?' I say.

'No word of a lie,' says Michael.

I smile at Michael, my friend, my soulmate.

Four of the Beckham Street Boyz cycle past us, doing wheelies. They shout to each other and then disappear off into the distance.

'When I get older and become a famous inventor,' says Michael, 'I'll get you your own fields for your animals to play in. Fields that don't have Beckham Street Boyz and T Crew anywhere near 'em.'

'That'd be good,' I say, grinning at him, the sun squinting my eyes.

Asbo's prickly rosettes are tickling my legs.

I snatch my courage again. 'Michael,' I say, 'I think Mr Richardson might be my dad.'

Michael spits out his bit of grass. 'ARE YOU FOR REAL? MR RICHARDSON?' shouts Michael. 'I am not coming to your house for tea if he's your dad. How can he be your dad?'.

'Stop shouting, Asbo, Chaos and Bob Marley don't like it. Mr Richardson wouldn't shout in front of animals, he rescued a spider and called it "my beauty" and he smiled at me when I signed his punishment book.'

Michael shuts his eyes and groans. 'I'm telling you, Nell, sometimes you are just too much. I thought you said Obo was your dad.'

'I've got to have options, Michael. I've got to find out who the real one is.'

A robin flutters above and lands on the window sill of the old youth club.

'Hold on to Asbo and Chaos,' I say, quickly sitting up. 'I need a better look at the robin to make sure he has no injuries. They're territorial like the T Crew and the Beckham Street Boyz, they fight another robin if it comes into their territory.' I creep up to the window sill, but it flies off just as I reach it.

The walls of the old youth club are cracked. They need repairing. I want to have a nose inside, so I pull myself up on the ledge. As I wipe the filthy window with my sleeve, memories flood me from when I was a little kid, about four years ago, peeping through this window. Sasha was renovating this Spitfire that used to live in the old youth club but she looked up and saw me, so I quickly scrambled down.

Through the window now I spy an old sofa, made up of wooden crates, covered in purple velvet. There are old, dusty pink and green cushions scattered on the floor, and cobwebs everywhere.

I pull the window, the catch gives way and up it comes. I wriggle inside, coughing in a cloud of dust.

'Odds fish, Nell, what you doing?' Michael calls. 'I can't hold Asbo and Chaos any more . . .'

I quickly throw the purple velvet on the floor, and make a pen with the wooden boxes. I grab the biggest to stand on, to peep out back at Michael.

'Come on in,' I say.

Michael hands Asbo and Chaos to me. I put them in the box pen, then he hands Bob Marley over to me. After putting him in the pen, I go back for Michael.

'Nell, supposing someone sees us,' whispers Michael.

'Since when's that stopped you?' I say. 'You're always getting caught. You spend most of your life in detention.'

'I'm only saying, Nell,' he says, as he climbs through the window.

We stand there, looking around us. Spiders and a few cockroaches scuttle across the floor, disappearing into corners. And then we just start running around laughing, and I feel free and it's the best feeling to feel like a kid just for once.

As I hold my arms out and whirl around, my face up to the ceiling, I notice a hatch like you get leading up to attics. There's a ladder lying on its side and an old broom.

'Michael, help me,' I say, grabbing one end of the ladder. 'I want to see what's up there.'

I shimmy up with the broom in one hand and ram it against the hatch door. It doesn't budge. Splinters of old white paint shower down around me, landing in Michael's hair. I do it again. Nothing. I do it again, and this time the door flicks up.

I pull myself up and there's the blue sky. I'm on the flat roof.

I crouch down to hold the top of the ladder for Michael.

'Michael, get up here,' I say.

'Oh, Nell, what if someone sees us? I don't like it.'

'Who's going to see us up here?' I say, but no sooner has he set both feet on the roof than I slam him down to the ground.

Chantal Smith is walking over the wasteland with Tanya.

Michael and I lie flat on our tummies and listen.

'I'm telling you, Chantal, Mr Samuels gotta let you be Nell Gwyn in the pageant.'

'My dad's taking me to Greenwich on Saturday to get my costume from my aunty's fancy dress shop. He says I'm his princess and when Mr Samuels sees my costume, he's bound to let me be Nell Gwyn.'

'Like there's even competition. Nell Hobs – what a joke!'

Michael gives my arm a squeeze. I shrug him off. I shut my eyes tight closed and bite my lip hard. As Chantal and Tanya cackle and walk past the youth club, and their voices become nothing more than whispers in the wind, I'm sure I can smell oranges. I jump up and shimmy back down the ladder, and then hold it for Michael.

He keeps giving me sympathy looks but I ignore him. I know he's trying to be kind but I don't want kind, I want action. Chantal's words – *I am going to be Nell Gwyn* – hop in my brain.

She can't be Nell Gwyn. I have to be . . . My dad – he might see me, and I need a dad and and . . . I can't keep on bothering Aunty Lou all the time, I just can't.

So I stand on my head in the corner of the youth club, watching all the upside-down insects scuttling around, till the blood rushes to my head and Chantal's words have gone.

'Michael, please will you look after my animal family at yours?' I say, landing on the floor and jumping back up. 'I got work to do.'

'Odds fish, I will,' says Michael and he holds his hand up for a high five.

'Odds fish,' I say as I slap his hand, then run back home.

I hammer on my door till Mum lets me in. She puts her hand on my arm but I shrug it off and storm past her, slamming my bedroom door shut. I get out my golden material and lay the costume book on my bed. I have a Nell Gwyn costume to make.

11

All Sunday I stay in my room, with the chair wedged under the door handle, trying to make my costume. I'm trying to sew the skirt part first.

But no matter what I do, I can't make it look like Nell Gwyn's dress in the costume book.

Mum keeps hammering on the door. 'Nell, let me in please. Why don't we collect your animal family from next door and have another party for two?'

I ignore her and carry on sewing. My heart beats like a hollow drum without my animal family, but I trust Michael to look after them.

Which is more than I trust my mum and her empty *pinkie promise*.

'Child, open the door now,' Aunty Lou tries next. 'I've got a nice piece of chicken, and rice, peas and gravy, and I've even done you some roast potatoes, crispy, just as you like them.'

My tummy rumbles but I don't answer. I jab my finger with the needle by mistake, for the hundred millionth time, and bite my lip to stop myself crying out. A drop of blood oozes on to the golden material.

I have got to get this costume finished. I grit my teeth with determination and pick up the needle again. Chantal Smith's not going to be Nell Gwyn. I am.

'Nell.' It's TJ. 'Got you some chips from Bernie's, he said I was to give you an extra big potion. He said, "We can't let poor Nelly starve."'

Can't let poor Nelly starve!

That's what King Charles II said on his death bed, about Nell Gwyn. *Let not poor Nelly starve*.

A flashback to all the times Bernie's smiled and waved at me, or told me to behave myself at school. I wonder if I should add Bernie from Bernie's Burger Bar to my dad list? I know him and Mum go way back.

The smell of chips wafts under the door. This is too much. I move the wedged chair, open the door a crack, shoot my hand out, grab the chips and slam the door shut before TJ can even blink.

'OK, Nell, I guess you want to be by yourself but you know where I am, right?'

I hear the front door slam as he leaves.

I wolf the chips like a piglet and the grease gets on my fingers and all over the material. I try to rub it off but it makes bigger greasy smudges.

Guinea pig singing trickles under the door.

'Nell, it's me. I've fed and watered your family but Chaos wants you. I know 'cause I'm an expert in guinea pig talk.'

I open the door to check on Chaos.

'Huh, I knew I could do it,' says Michael, puffing out his chest. 'I told 'em I could get you to come out, huh! What yer doing, Nell?'

'Nothing.'

'Can I come in?'

'No, wait there.'

I gently take Chaos from him and shut the door.

The little cream guinea pig nestles into my shoulder. Then I put her on my bed to have a run around but she runs straight over to the costume material, and nibbles it, and bits of sawdust that were attached to her fur stick to the grease splodges on the material. Making costumes with a guinea pig on the bed is impossible. I open the door and hand Chaos back to Michael.

'Asbo will be missing her. Thanks,' I say.

'Use the walkie-talkie, Nell, if your mum goes out later.'

'I promise,' I say.

'No word of a lie,' says Michael.

'No word of a lie,' I say.

'Odds fish,' we say together and we link thumbs.

I shut the door and shake the golden costume material out in horror. It's a greasy, sawdusty, mucky mess.

'Nell, please come out.' It's Mum again.

Angry tears prickle my eyes.

'*Ride a cock-horse to Banbury Cross to see a fine lady upon a white horse.*'

She's saying our special nursery rhyme, the one she used to say to me when I was a little kid, but I ignore her. My mouth feels so dry I screw the scrumpled, yucky gold material into the bottom of my rucksack and shut it behind a door in my mind.

I close my eyes.

The crowds are pushing and shoving to get into the theatre. Men in big brimmed hats with feathers. Ladies in fine silken dresses with jewellery on that sparkles. I'm getting pushed and shoved as I try and try to get to my theatre seat. Then I see her, a very young Nell Gwyn, in a blue dress, carrying a basket of sweet-looking oranges that are covered in leaves.

'Oranges, sixpence for a sweet orange. Who will buy my oranges? You'll have one, won't you, sir?' she says to a tall gentleman dressed in high leather boots, gloves, bronze silk breeches and golden cape. Then Nell Gwyn turns and sees me and smiles and laughs her pretty laugh, and she picks the sweetest-looking orange and reaches out and gives it to me.

'That'll quench your thirst, my little one,' she says, and I break the skin and bite into it and a river of sweet juices trickle down my dry throat.

Nell Gwyn turns to me, winks and blows me a kiss.

On Monday, as I walk past Bernie's Burger Bar on the way to school, I pop my head round the door. He's unloading a box of bottled water and has his back to me. I look at the framed photograph on the wall behind the counter of Bernie, his wife and six little Bernies – four girls and two boys. They all have black hair like me! Maybe I could stay at theirs when the demon drink gets Mum. Bernie and his wife have so many kids, they wouldn't notice one more. I imagine myself standing on my head in the middle of the photograph. I would fit in very nicely into their family, I think. Bernie turns and sees me and throws me a bottle of water.

'Get some of that down you, it's good for you. I heard about you locking yourself in your bedroom, you had everyone worried.'

I smile my best, most daughter-like smile and am just drawing breath to question him on any night out he might've had with my mum twelve or so years ago, when his phone rings.

'I asked for three boxes of Sprite, two boxes of Coke and one of Tango,' Bernie yells into the phone. 'and what've you given me? Four boxes of water! I WANT TO SPEAK TO THE MANAGER, THIS IS THE FOURTH TIME YOU'VE MESSED MY ORDER UP.'

I sneak out of the shop. My throat feels dry, so I gulp some water. It's important for us naturalists to keep hydrated.

I walk to school with hot, dry, scratchy hands and eyes, and heavy, thuddy feet.

As I crawl through the forbidden gap in the hedge by the old girls' changing rooms I stop to watch a colony of ants carrying a bit of apple to their nest, working as a team, like we do during *Operation Ark*.

I've missed registration (again!) so I go straight to history class.

There's a red X on the door of our classroom and a sign that says, *ABANDON HOPE ALL YE WHO ENTER HERE*. I feel a bit anxious, I'm not sure what to do, so I stand on my head in the corridor for a minute, before pushing the handle of the classroom door down slowly, and peeping round.

When the boys see me, they start rolling their eyes and making gagging noises and falling off their chairs. All the class have red blotches drawn on their cheeks, except for Chantal Smith, who's sitting there filing her nails.

'She thinks just 'cause she's Nell Gwyn in the pageant she can be late, sir,' says Chantal.

'Yeah, that's taking liberties if you ask me, sir,' says Tanya.

'*Take no heed of their spite,*' whispers Nell Gwyn in my ear, as clear as anything, and there she is standing before me in her gold dress. She puts her fingers to her lips, creeps up to Tanya and stands over her looking down at her blue fringe.

'*Has she dipped her hair in the ink pot?*' says Nell Gwyn, her tinkling laugh making me dissolve into giggles.

'Just who do you think you're laughing at?' says Tanya.

'No one,' I say, giving her one of my *don't mess with me* looks.

'Ah, come in, Nell,' says Mr Samuels with a smile. 'It's 1665, the time of the Great Plague.'

I smile back, 'cause you can't help but smile at Mr Samuels.

Michael is flopped over the desks, his tongue lolling out of his mouth.

I shove him over, so I can sit down.

'Nell, get off me. I'm dying of the plague, you can't go shoving me, it's disrespectful.'

'Ah, but that's exactly what they did,' says Mr Samuels. 'The dead bodies would all be shoved on top of each other, piled in a cart by a man ringing a bell, shouting, "BRING OUT YOUR DEAD." He would stop at the doors with a red cross painted on, with *Lord have mercy on us* written above in white, because this meant that a plague victim lay inside the house dead or dying.'

'I think Bernie from Bernie's Burgers could be my dad,' I whisper in Michael's ear.

'Good, we'll get free chips,' says Michael, and just carries on pretending to die of the plague. And, no word of a lie, that's all he has to say to my big bit of news.

'The plague was actually caused by fleas,' says Mr Samuels.

'Sir,' I say, 'fleas are most interesting creatures. They live on blood but they can survive a hundred days without a blood dinner. And they can jump 150 times their own height, which is like me being able to jump over the Beckham Estate.'

'Very interesting, Nell, thank you for sharing that,' says Mr Samuels.

'Nell knows so much about them 'cause she's most probably got fleas,' whispers Chantal, loud enough for me to hear.

I feel myself exploding inside and I'm just about to launch myself at Chantal but I feel *Nell Gwyn's lips brush my cheek*.

I tune in to Mr Samuels again.

'They killed all the dogs and cats because they thought they were spreading the plague,' says Mr Samuels, 'but that only made things worse, as it meant that there were no dogs and cats to kill the rats. It was the fleas on the rats that caused the plague.'

I stare at Mr Samuels in horror. They killed all the dogs and cats!

'Sir, sir, what was Nell Gwyn doing during the plague?' I ask.

'No one knows for sure, Nell, it's not been recorded. She would've been fifteen years old during the plague. The theatres were closed, so she wouldn't have had any work.'

I knew where she was with all my heart. She was rescuing the dogs and cats.

'In 1666 was the Great Fire of London, which started in a baker's shop in Pudding Lane,' says Mr Samuels.

'All the baker's family got out except for the maid, who was the first person to die in the fire.'

As Mr Samuels talks about King Charles II riding on horseback, helping people, my lids start to droop.

I jolt as Michael nudges me in the ribs. I stretch my eyes wide to stop them closing but my bones feel heavy with Mum worries. I really, really want to stand on my head but I can't, not in the middle of a history class.

Mr Samuels's voice washes over me . . . 'Families fleeing the city with all that they owned in a cart . . . The houses being wooden and close together . . . the fire spread. The king ordered houses to be pulled down so that the fire couldn't reach over the gaps . . . The people loved him . . .' *Loved him . . . loved hiiiiiim . . .*

Nell Gwyn scuttles down Drury Lane, past the houses with red crosses on the doors.

She shudders as a big black rat runs over her foot. Hearing a tiny mew, she turns to see a tiny black kitten cowering in a doorway with a red cross upon its door. Nell scoops the little kitten up. She checks that she isn't being followed and sneaks into the deserted theatre and into her dressing room, where all the other dogs and cats she's rescued are waiting for the scraps she has brought to feed her animal family.

The barking and meowing get louder and louder. The city fills with flames, King Charles rides by on a white horse, Nell Gwyn behind him, clutching on to his coat. I run out into the road. 'I'm here,' I call. The horse rears, its hooves pawing the air.

'Nell, Nell, Nell, wake up.'

It's Miss Petunia. The classroom's empty, apart from Mr Samuels, who's sitting at his desk, looking at me with worried eyes.

12

Miss Petunia arranged for me to sleep in the medical room all afternoon. There's a school calendar on the wall. On it marked in red is *Year 7 parents' evening*. I run my finger along the weeks and count. One, two, three. It's in four weeks' time, just before half term.

Miss Petunia comes in and catches me with my finger still on the calendar and smiles.

'Is your mum coming to see you get your nature prize?'

My tummy catapults up to my tonsils.

'Yes, miss,' I say, but inside I'm thinking, *Supposing she doesn't, supposing she's out on the razz and the demon's captured her*, and the pain of that thought's too much, so I say quickly, 'She'll come unless she's busy.'

Miss Petunia looks really sad as she hands me a mug of hot chocolate.

'Thanks, miss,' I say. 'I've kept it secret, miss. I've told no one, not even Michael.'

'Good,' says Miss Petunia, 'and the hot chocolate is *my* secret, it's from my top secret stash.' She taps the side of her nose with her finger.

'Nell,' says Miss Petunia in her most gentle voice. 'Didn't you sleep last night? Is there anything you would like to talk about?'

And I want to talk, I really want to tell her about being scared every second of the day that Mum is safe. But the words freeze on my lips.

I shake my head, I can't risk people knowing in case I get sent away. I can't leave my animal family, I just can't.

I shake my head and close my eyes.

I hear her sigh as she shuts the door behind her.

When she's gone I stand on my head, on the bed, with my feet against the wall, till the blood rushes to my brain, and I can't think any more about the Borough Nature Prize and will or won't Mum be there, or the fact that I won't be able to be Nell Gwyn in the pageant, 'cause I don't have a decent costume. I crash back on to the bed and curl up into a tight ball and I shut my eyes on my world and never want to open them again.

13

No word of a lie, the next day I get told off seven times at school for not concentrating.

Finally, after a day that seemed like a year, I reach the last class of the day: maths. Mrs Hubert's droning on about something or other and everyone's scribbling down sums, except for Michael, who's tugging at a screw on his chair and writing in his invention book.

I've torn out a page from my maths book and under my desk I'm writing down my list of possible dads while trying not to feel sick at the thought of my costume for the pageant.

Obo
Mr Richardson
Bernie from Bernie's Burger Bar

Out of the corner of my eye *I am sure I spy Nell Gwyn, asleep in the corner from maths-induced boredom.*

I hear Chantal whispering plans for a sleepover with Tanya.

'I'll show you my Nell Gwyn costume, Tanya. I'll even let you try it on.'

'Oh, thank you, Chantal.'

'And, I'll do you your nails, Tanya, 'cause you've got to stop biting them, 'cause that's what friends do, they go to each other's houses and they do each other's nails,' and she turns round and gives me a proper dirty look.

'Chantal Smith, why are you talking? I hope it's about the maths problems. Would you like to share your mathematical genius with the rest of the class, hmmm? WELL, I AM WAITING!' bellows Mrs Hubert.

There's a bang.

Michael is on the floor, in a heap of wood.

There's a horror-shock of silence, then me and my whole class are literally rolling on the floor with Michael, laughing. It takes Mrs Hubert ten minutes to stop us having the hysterics.

'But, Mrs Hubert,' says Michael, 'I was doing a maths problem, I was working out how many nuts and bolts it takes to hold my desk and chair together, and doing an equation at the same time, working out the ratio of how few nuts and bolts it would need for me to keep balance on the chair.'

'Well, you found your answer, didn't you?' says Mrs Hubert.

'Yes, miss, I did,' says Michael.

'You were meant to be doing the equation on the whiteboard.'

'But they were too easy,' says Michael.

She gives him one of her poison looks. 'Detention, Michael,' she says.

The bell goes for the end of class.

I link my thumb with Michael's.

'Odds fish,' we both say together, and then he snatches up his briefcase, and rushes off to sign the punishment book, before going to detention.

I tip my books and pencil case into my rucksack, but it comes open again and my pens roll all over the floor. I'm on my hands and knees picking them up as my class stumble over me in their rush to get home.

I hear a gasp. *Nell Gwyn stands by the door of the empty classroom, with her hand over her mouth, staring wide-eyed at something.*

I scramble up to see Chantal with my screwed-up attempt at a Nell Gwyn costume between her thumb and first finger, her nose scrunched up, like it smells.

'GIVE THAT BACK!' I shout.

'Is *this* your costume?' asks Chantal, laughing.

Tanya's standing by the door on look-out.

'I SAID, GIVE IT BACK NOW!'

'It's all creased and dirty like you,' yells Tanya.

'Do you really think Mr Samuels'll let you be Nell Gwyn wearing a dirty piece of creased-up material? In your dreams, Nell Hobs.'

I lunge at her, grabbing the material. There's a ripping sound.

'LOOK WHAT YOU'VE DONE!' I scream. *A faint scent of oranges fills my nostrils and I feel Nell Gwyn's hand in mine.* I look up and Mr Richardson's staring through the classroom window. He marches past Tanya and into the room.

'What's going on here?' he says.

'Nothing, Mr Richardson,' says Chantal.

'It doesn't look like nothing.'

He gives Chantal and Tanya one of his stares. 'I've got my eye on both of you. Especially you, Chantal Smith. Now go home.'

They slink out of the classroom.

'What's this, Nell?' he says, nodding to the material.

'Nothing, sir, it's just some material left over from a bridesmaid dress my mum wore.'

'Lovely colour,' he says, 'like the colour on a goldfinch's wing.'

Mr Richardson really is a naturalist. 'Thank you, sir,' I say, shoving the material back in my rucksack.

'Nell,' he says, 'if you're being bullied, or if you want to talk, my door's always open. And, as I said, if you want to bring your mum in for a chat . . .'

'Thank you, Mr Richardson, sir,' I blurt out, almost shouting. 'I am quite all right thank you very much.' And I run, run, run out of school, jam jars clanking in my rucksack.

14

I ring my doorbell, wondering what I'm going to find. Mum opens the door so quickly she must've been waiting just the other side. She's wearing a flowery dress that I haven't seen before, a cardigan, no make-up and her hair is scraped back in a ponytail.

'Nelly,' she says, giving me a hug and a kiss on the cheek, 'I'm so looking forward to hearing about what you learned at school today.' She pulls me through to my bedroom, where my animal family greet me with chats and squeaks. On my bed is a pile of washed and ironed clothes.

'I was just putting your things away.'

I grab a pair of my jeans to hang in the wardrobe.

'No, I'll do it,' she says, taking them from me. 'Look in there.' And she nods to a carrier bag that is leaning against the wardrobe.

Inside are packets of gerbil food, hamster food, a

tub of fish food, a packet of guinea pig pellets and a selection of fresh vegetables, for Bob Marley and all my rodents.

'Mum, how . . . ?'

'I got a job,' says Mum, clapping her hands, 'well, just for a few hours here and there. Bernie's having nightmares with his orders and is paying me to sort the stockroom out and get on the phone to make sure they deliver what he actually asked for, that sort of thing. I started this morning.'

Bernie must really care about us if he's given her a job. He's a much better dad option than Mr Richardson.

'Oh, Mum, I'm so proud of you.' I hug her.

Mum must've had about twenty different jobs, but they never last long.

'Bernie was asking about you,' says Mum, 'ever so interested, he was, in how you're doing at school.'

I feel my face cracking into the biggest smile ever. Bernie's taking an interest in my education, just like a dad would.

'Mum, did you and Bernie ever go to parties and things, before I was born?'

'Yeah, course. Bernie's a right laugh.'

My heart literally feels like it will explode as I

think about the possibility of Bernie being my dad.

I feed my animal family and change into the freshly washed clothes that Mum's left out for me. As I follow her into the kitchen I stumble over a plank of wood that's leaning against the wall.

'Oh, mind yourself,' says Mum. 'Obo dropped that round, ready for when he puts up the shelves for me.'

So that's what the kiss and the promise on the scrap of paper I found meant! Obo's going to make shelves which, if you ask me, is a very dad type thing to do. Maybe he could fix our flat and fix Mum.

Suddenly I've lots of potential dads to consider.

'Look,' says Mum and points to our dinner, which is laid out on the table. Everything on the table is green, no word of a lie.

Lettuce and rocket and, well, just green stuff. There's even a bowl of green apples for dessert. If she carries on like this, I may have to go to Bernie's Burger Bar for nutrition.

There a banging on the door. It's Michael, home from detention.

'COME QUICK, NELL, THE TADPOLES ARE GROWING LEGS!'

Aunty Lou is coming along the balcony, a

shopping bag in each hand. 'Michael, what are you shouting about?'

'THE TADPOLES ARE GROWING LEGS, AUNTY LOU!'

Aunty Lou puts down her shopping bags on our doorstep and laughs and claps her hands. 'Well, that's a cause for celebration. Manners, Michael, what did I tell you to ask Stacey and Nell before I popped to the shops?'

'Oh, yes,' says Michael. 'We would be very pleased if both of you would join us for dinner.'

Mum says, 'Oh! That would be lovely, but our dinner's on the table.'

I bite the words back to beg and plead for us to go to Aunty Lou's, so I can try and have an evening off from watching over Mum.

Aunty Lou and Michael step through our front door, walk into our kitchen and look at our tea. There's the longest pause before Aunty Lou says, 'Oh, Stacey, it looks lovely, you have been working hard. It's, erm . . . very green . . .'

'Bob Marley would like it,' says Michael.

I take a sharp breath. 'Michael,' I hiss.

But Mum bends double and laughs so hard she's shaking. 'I've made my daughter tortoise food for dinner! What was I thinking . . . ?'

'We can use it for a little side salad,' says Aunty Lou.

'And some for Bob Marley,' says Michael.

'Bob Marley can have some if he so wishes,' says Aunty Lou. 'Bring it come, it will not go to waste, join us for a nice bit of curry goat and rice and peas.'

'Nell, come, look,' Michael says, and we all run to his room and stick our heads out of the window to look at the little tadpoles swimming in the tank on his window ledge, some now with the teeniest of tiny legs. No word of a lie, it's one of the most interesting naturalist observations I've ever seen in my whole life. Even Mum, who is not a naturalist in the slightest, looks at the little tadpoles swimming with wonder in her eyes.

I hear the door open behind me.

'Eyes tight shut, Nell.' It's TJ. He puts his hand over my eyes so there's no peeking. 'I've got a surprise for you,' and he guides me out of Michael's room and into his bedroom. I hear everyone else following.

'Ta da!' he says and takes his hand off my eyes and there's the most beautiful new tortoise table I've ever seen, with plants and rocks and a lamp to keep Bob Marley warm, and a little pool for a drink and a dip. TJ's thought of everything.

'I made it for your little tortoise man,' he says.

I'm so choked at his kindness that tears itch my eyes, and I fling my arms round TJ and hug him.

'But I don't understand,' Mum says, 'it's very nice but Nell already has a tortoise table.'

Slowly, slowly, I let go, 'cause I realise what this tortoise table means.

It's an *Operation Ark* tortoise table, for the rescue of Bob Marley, if Mum goes out drinking.

I look round and drink in the awkward silence in the room.

TJ looks horrified at the realisation of what he's done; Michael's biting his lip. Aunty Lou has her hand on Mum's shoulder and Mum, well, she just looks bewildered.

Then I see the ding of understanding ping her brain as she looks round at the horror on our faces.

Mum laughs, walks over to TJ and kisses him on the cheek.

'Thank you for your kindness to my Nelly.' She winks at me. 'I guess you can never have too many tortoise tables. I am going to get Bob Marley, so he can enjoy exploring his second home,' she says, and then runs out of the room.

I sink down on TJ's bed.

'I'm sorry, Nell,' he says, 'I didn't . . .'

'TJ, it's OK. 'Cause we all know that at any time she might . . .'

Aunty Lou kisses the top of my head. 'I'm going to start cooking,' she says. 'TJ, your handiwork's beautiful. I'm so proud.'

I spend time looking around TJ's room and see that the wardrobe door is fixed back on and TJ's wall of trainer boxes is neatly stacked against the wall. Michael is standing in front like he is guarding them. Mum's taking her time. Supposing . . . My anxieties start to rise.

But then the door opens and in she comes, carrying Bob Marley. She places him in his new tortoise table. 'There you go, Bob Marley, have adventures exploring your new home,' she says, and then goes to help Aunty Lou. Soon I can hear them deep in conversation.

Words like, 'You've got the strength inside you, Stacey,' and, 'You're doing so well' drift to my ears as yummy cooking smells drift up my nostrils.

TJ, Michael and me watch Bob Marley go for a dip

in his new pool. I reckon he's excited by his new home, only he's too cool to show it.

Aunty Lou brings in some of Mum's green stuff for Bob Marley. 'Wash your hands,' she says to us, 'then come to the table for our celebration supper.'

And so we do and as we sit round the table enjoying our curry goat, celebrating my tadpoles' new legs, I'm watching Mum all the time. *Be strong this time, Mum, please*, I say my silent prayer over and over again as she pours herself a glass of water and chats to Michael about his inventions.

'Strawberries and cream, to celebrate Bob Marley's new tortoise table,' says Aunty Lou.

And we laugh and chat and eat strawberries.

I feel something warm against my foot. Napoleon leaps on the table, knocking Mum's drinking glass over and, as it smashes on the kitchen floor, the noise shatters through my bones and I'm shaking and I can't stop, 'cause Mum's like that glass and I am just waiting for her to shatter, and I want to stand on my head, but I can't, 'cause there's broken glass and water everywhere.

'Get that cat away from the food!' says Aunty Lou, leaping out of her chair.

'NAPOLEON!' yells Mum, scooping him off the

table, before he can jump down and cut himself. She takes him from the room, and I hear her put him out of the front door.

I feel a hand on my still shaking arm.

'She doing well, Nelly,' says Aunty Lou. 'Come on now, you can't be watching her day and night.'

'But I have to, Aunty Lou, I . . .' I swallow my words as Mum comes back into the kitchen.

'This has been so kind of you,' says Mum. 'I insist on clearing the broken glass and doing the dishes.'

'What homework have you two got?' asks Aunty Lou.

'GEOGRAPHY,' groans Michael.

'Geography is very important,' says Aunty Lou, 'especially for you, Michael, since finding your way on time to your own school seems to be a problem.'

We all laugh and Aunty Lou lets us into her special front room as a treat. It's where she keeps her Mary and baby Jesus figurines and the glass angels on display. She puts a plastic sheet down on the carpet, and Michael and I lie on our bellies on top of it. Aunty Lou gets out her old atlas that she used at school in Jamaica, and she does what she always does when she supervises our homework, she confiscates Michael's invention book till he's finished.

'Mr Boswell said we've got to write about the River Mersey, in Liverpool,' I say, and I start to draw a picture and write about the Atlantic grey seals, bottlenose dolphins and harbour porpoise that sometimes swim in from the Irish Sea. I don't stop, even when Napoleon stalks back into the room, and lies down right across the map of Liverpool in Aunty Lou's old atlas, and reaches out his paw to bat my pen as I try to write.

'That cat,' says Aunty Lou, 'causing chaos and mayhem.' But she doesn't shoo him out. She knows that Napoleon's an unofficial member of my animal family and his purrs calm my anxieties.

I hear Mum singing that Beyoncé song about haloes from the kitchen. When I've coloured in the last bit of the River Mersey, and the last dish has been washed, dried and put away, Mum helps me pack my school rucksack, and we go hand in hand back home.

As I have a soak in the bath and clean my teeth ready for bed, I want so much to remind Mum of her *pinkie promise* to make my Nell Gwyn costume, but I *don't* want to remind her of our party for two, when she first gave me the golden material and then ran out on me, into the rain . . . I'm so scared that she'll do it again, so I think it's best if I leave the gold material hidden in the bottom of my rucksack.

That night, Michael checks up on me through the walkie-talkie.

'*Odds fish,*' he says. '*Nell, are you OK?*'

I run over to my walkie-talkie. '*Odds fish,*' I say. '*Michael, I really hope with all my heart this time she stops for good.*'

'*I think this time she will,*' says Michael. '*I got a feeling.*'

'*No word of a lie,*' I say.

'*No word of a lie,*' he says. '*Odds fish, over and out.*'

'*Odds fish, over and out,*' I say back. Then I creep to Mum's bedroom, just to check she's still there.

I hold my breath and open the door a crack but she's there sleeping, looking like a little girl, dream thoughts creeping across her face in the dark.

After I've checked her breathing I go back to my room and stand on my head before I go to sleep and *Nell Gwyn teases my dreams, dancing a jig through my mind, whirling my fantasies of summer days and fathers around and around.*

* * *

And that's how we are, Mum and me, for the next four weeks. I bury my Nell Gwyn costume worries deep, deep in my brain and I keep telling myself the only thing that matters is Mum not drinking and that she'll be OK to see me get the Borough Nature Prize at parents' evening, which is getting closer and closer. During that time the tadpoles become the teeniest of tiny frogs and Michael, Mum, Aunty Lou, Buster and me release them in a pond on Parliament Hill Fields. Buster is most puzzled by the proceedings and puts his nose next to a little frog on a stone. The tiny frog jumps and Buster jumps in the air too. We all laugh, and Mum treats us all to Nando's to celebrate the frogs' release into their natural habitat. It's good being the only naturalist on the Beckham Estate.

15

The day of parents' evening arrives. Mum makes me a boiled egg and toast soldiers for breakfast.

'Mum, remember parents' evening is at 5.30 tonight. You won't be late, will you?'

'Nell,' she says, '*pinkie promise* that I won't be late.'

'*Pinkie promise*,' I say and we link our little fingers with love.

'See you tonight.' Mum hands me a packed lunch and waves me goodbye. I keep turning and looking at her on the step, waving and waving, getting smaller and smaller, as I walk away. I wish that moment could last for ever.

Despite the fact that on my safari to school I only stop once, to move a caterpillar from a dry old branch to one with more leaves in a safer location,

I still have somehow managed to miss registration. Miss Gordon tuts at me. I ignore her as I've got more important things to worry about. She marks me in the register and points to a notice on her door that says:

YEAR 7 please go to maths first period.
History teachers in meeting

Rubbish! That means boring maths. I spy through the crack in the door the history teachers all squashed into Mr Richardson's office. Mr Samuels is munching on a chocolate digestive, a mug of tea in his hand. I hear words like 'make the mayor welcome' and 'greet the photographer from *North West London Tonight* newspaper'.

North West London Tonight! I feel like there are a hundred million butterflies fluttering in my tummy. No word of a lie, every single family in this part of London must get that newspaper. Obo, Bernie or Mr Richardson'll be so proud to have a daughter in *North West London Tonight* for winning the Borough Nature Prize that they might claim me. Or if they are not my dads, well, someone, somewhere might see my picture and realise who I am and call the newspaper, and I might even end up on TV and and . . .

Clickety clack footsteps, a tap on my shoulder. It's Miss Petunia looking stern, but with a twinkle in her eye.

'Nell Hobs, shouldn't you be in class?'

'Yes, miss, maths, miss.'

'Is your mum coming to parents' evening?'

'Yes, Miss Petunia,' I say.

Miss Petunia bends forwards and whispers, 'She won't be disappointed then, will she?' She winks.

'No, miss,' I say, and inside I pray that Mum will be so proud and happy when she sees me win the Borough Nature Prize that the demon will tempt her no more.

'Hurry to your class now,' says Miss Petunia, in a teacher voice, then whispers, 'If you hurry you'll get there before Mrs Hubert. She's been held up as the photocopier jammed in the staff room.'

'Thanks, miss,' I say.

It says in *Creepy Crawly Fact or Fiction* that butterflies emerging from a chrysalis have to wait for their wings to fill with blood before they can fly, but I don't wait for anything. My feet literally fly down the corridor to maths faster than any butterfly.

The classroom door swings open.

Michael's standing there, holding the door with a fixed smile on his face. 'Good morning Mrs—' His face falls as he realises it's me.

'Oh, it's you, Nell. Quick, out of the way.'

And he actually shoves me! Michael's shirt's tucked in, his tie is in a tidy knot, and his shoes are polished.

Footsteps are coming down the corridor. Michael quickly shuts the door, so he can open it again when Mrs Hubert walks in.

'Good morning, Mrs Hubert, and how are you this fine morning?' says Michael, with a false smile plastered on his face.

I'm confused for a moment, but then it hits me. PARENTS' EVENING! Michael's for it when Mrs Hubert talks to Aunty Lou about all his detentions. I get the giggles then. Mrs Hubert looks Michael up and down.

'Sit down, Michael,' she says, without even thanking him.

When Michael opens the door for Mr Samuels for our postponed history lesson, well, sir just laughs and fills the room with joy. Mr Samuels hands Michael a letter, which he quickly reads, grins at sir, then stuffs in his briefcase.

All day, Michael runs around, carrying bags for teachers, whether they want him to or not. He looks properly funny walking down the corridor with Miss Petunia's handbag.

'Oh, it suits you, Michael – goes with you shoes,' shouts out one of the Beckham Street Boyz from year ten. A group of them are loitering by the toilets.

The rest of the Boyz all crack up and start wolf-whistling and hollering, 'Like your handbag, Prof M.' But Michael don't care, he's on a mission.

Michael's antics are a good distraction from my own thoughts, but they still keep kicking into my brain.

PLEASE, Mum, be on time, I pray. My anxieties take over my heart, brain and soul and I start thinking, *Supposing Mum's late, and supposing the teachers guess about Mum and I get sent away from my animal family*. Then I get a grip and banish those anxieties and think happy thoughts of me being awarded the Borough Nature Prize. Of Mum being so proud that her demon will pack its bags and leave our lives for ever. Me with my picture in *North West London Tonight* and my dad, whoever he may be, crying, saying, 'That's my daughter.'

The stress of my battling thoughts is doing my head in, and I obviously can't stand on my head in my lessons, so I flop over in my chair with my head between my knees, whenever my teachers aren't looking.

After what seems like a century, the bell for the end of the last lesson rings. The dinner ladies are staying late, and put out pizza slices and bowls of salad for year seven to eat as we wait for our mums and dads. I can't eat any pizza, even though it's my favourite – thin crust, with chicken, peppers and mushroom topping. I can't even eat one bite.

If only I had a dad like King Charles II. I drift off as I *imagine King Charles, as he rides up to school in his golden carriage with four black horses for parents' evening. His horses gallop through a puddle, splashing Chantal Smith – who is a lowly begger in the street – from head to toe. King Charles leaps out of his carriage and marches me in to see Mrs Hubert, and she kneels down and kisses King Charles's silver buckled shoes.*

'*Your Majesty, it is an honour to teach your daughter Nell, and we are all so proud of her for being the only naturalist on the Beckham Estate.*'

'*You must make their lessons fun, Mrs Hubert, or*

I shall banish you from the kingdom of north west London,' says King Charles.

Mrs Hubert scrabbles off her knees when she spies Aunty Lou, to run and tell her about Michael's detentions, but Nell Gwyn, who is providing the entertainment for parents' evening, dances a jig with Aunty Lou, and makes her so happy that she pushes Mrs Hubert out of the way as she tries to whisper nasty things about Michael into her ear. Nell Gwyn winks at me, blows me a kiss, then disappears.

'Nell, Nell, are you all right?' It's Mr Samuels.

'Yes, sir,' I say.

The school assembly hall is empty of kids; even Michael's abandoned me. Only teachers remain, sitting at tables, with signs saying their names and subjects.

There's a red velvet notice board with a sign that says *Some former pupils we are very proud of.* I immediately spot a photograph of TJ – underneath it says: *Studying to be a car mechanic.* That should keep Aunty Lou happy. Sasha smiles down at me from another photograph, looking beautiful wearing a red dress. Underneath it says: *Now studying performing arts.*

I also spot Willem from our estate, who lives with his Gran Gracie who's Aunty Lou's best friend. His photo says: *Now attending a course for gifted mathematicians*.

There's a table covered in a blue cloth displaying all the trophies. When I realise one of those is going to be mine, my heart flutters as fast as pigeons' wings.

'Everyone's outside waiting for their parents,' says Mr Samuels.

I nod and drift into the playground but everyone's pushing and shoving each other to get to their families.

Rulla, the head girl, is standing by the doorway, greeting parents as they arrive. 'I feel like turning a cartwheel,' she whispers into my ear as I pass, and gives my hand a gentle squeeze.

'Mum, Dad,' my classmates yell, walking over to their parents as they come through the school gate, and then look embarrassed as their parents hug them.

Don't they even realise how lucky they are to get a dad hug? Chantal, who doesn't look a bit embarrassed and of course always, always has to be the centre of attention, runs up to her dad, squealing as he swings her round.

'Hello, princess,' he says to her, and they walk inside, his arm round her shoulder. I try not to stare, but I can't help it. I feel a punch-pain in my tummy as I watch them. Chantal looks back at me and I quickly look away.

I stand on my tiptoes searching for Mum.

Please come, please, please, I pray over and over. More and more mums and dads walk through the school gate. My heart stops every time I catch a glimpse of blonde hair, but it's never Mum. I just can't take it any more, so I stand on my head in the playground.

Gradually, the playground empties, till it's just me and Michael. Then Aunty Lou emerges from the darkening evening shadows. But still no Mum . . . I crash land in a heap.

'She *pinkie promised* me, Aunty Lou, I thought that this time . . .'

Aunty Lou looks at me and sighs.

'Get on your feet, child, you're all flushed.' And she pulls a comb out of her bag, and starts attacking my curls, but I don't even feel the pain of the tugs through my numbness.

'I knocked and knocked on your door,' says Aunty Lou, 'but she didn't answer. So I guess you're stuck with me.' As she kisses me on the cheek, my heart hits the playground with a thud.

We follow Aunty Lou into the hall. She smiles as she sees TJ's photograph, looks around, then bustles us over to Mrs Hubert's table.

Michael looks so scared. Mrs Hubert takes a deep breath and then starts listing every single detention and the reason behind it. She must've spent ages memorising them all, I think, as she goes on and on and on.

'And another thing,' she says. 'Michael does his own thing, rather than do the exercises I have set the class.'

Mrs Hubert picks up Michael's maths book, and shows Aunty Lou all the diagrams and numbers scrawled all over the pages.

'Mrs Hubert,' says Aunty Lou, 'I will be having words with Michael about his behaviour but I assume that you became a teacher because you have an interest in the world of mathematics? Well, what a gift and a challenge for you as a teacher to have a pupil like Michael, who's so fascinated that he immerses himself completely in the world of science and numbers. He's just hungry for you to captivate him and teach him new things. Now, can we talk about Nell, please? How is she doing with her mathematics?'

Michael and I stare at Aunty Lou in awe as Mrs Hubert deflates like a balloon.

'I should talk to Nell's mother about Nell,' says Mrs Hubert.

'Well, as her mother's been unavoidably detained and it's usually me who supervises her homework, I would be grateful if you could tell me how she is doing.'

'That's 'cause Michael and I do our homework together, Mrs Hubert,' I blurt out, 'cause I don't want Mrs Hubert getting suspicious.

'Nell has a nasty habit of tearing out pages in her maths book,' says Mrs Hubert, flicking through my exercise book, to show Aunty Lou all the places I have done this. 'Oh, and Michael does it too,' she says, showing the ripped page at the back of his book.

'No, that was me,' I say. 'It wasn't Michael.'

'Why, child?' asks Aunty Lou.

''Cause I needed paper,' I say.

I sink lower in the chair as 'could try harder', 'struggles with this subject', 'always late' swim over my head.

Aunty Lou marches us to teacher after teacher: English, Spanish, geography.

They all say the same thing. 'Nell always looks tired', 'Nell daydreams', 'Nell could try harder', but I'm not paying attention. My eyes are still searching for Mum. She *pinkie promised*. Maybe she's in the bath and didn't hear Aunty Lou knocking. Maybe there's been a power cut, and she couldn't charge her phone, and doesn't realise the time. She has to see me getting the Borough Nature Prize, she just has to, then everything will be all right.

The queue to see Miss Petunia is too long, so Aunty Lou drags us over to Mr Samuels and plonks herself in front of him. I can see the anger sparks dancing off her.

'Well,' she says, 'I suppose you're going to tell me that Michael and Nell are in their own world and do not achieve anything whatsoever in your lesson.'

'I can say that if you want me to?' Mr Samuels says, twinkling at her. 'But actually I was going to tell you that you could not wish to find two more delightful children. They're a joy and an honour to teach.'

There's a silence as Aunty Lou gapes at him with an open mouth, and then she begins to laugh. Mr

Samuels joins in and they laugh together like mad people. Michael rolls his eyes at me.

'In fact, I'd like Michael to be Ki—'

Miss Petunia claps her hands.

'Ladies and gentlemen, if I could have your attention please. I've just been told that the mayor's arrived, so as our parents' evening draws to an end, I would like you all to take your seats for this evening's prizegiving.'

'No, not yet!' I cry. I didn't realise I had said it out loud. People are staring at me.

Please, Mum, come, I pray inside. *Please see me get my prize*.

Everyone hurries over to the rows of seats that have been laid out in front of the stage, jostling for a good place.

Aunty Lou, Michael and I are in the back row. When everyone is seated Mr Richardson, accompanied by Mayor Felicity Cordour, walks down the central aisle between our chairs. The mayor is wearing a glamorous pink coat, with her gold mayor necklace, and looks like a film star. Behind them scuttles a black spiky-haired photographer.

Mr Richardson waffles on introducing Felicity Cordour but I'm not looking or listening, my head is swivelling round, looking at the door behind me. *Please, Mum, please, you* pinkie promised.

Miss Petunia stands up and starts to announce the winner of each award. The mayor hands out the prizes for English, then maths, then geography as we applaud, but there's still no Mum.

'Now it's time for two special awards,' announces Miss Petunia.

'Please, Mum, please come,' I whisper over and over.

'First, I would like to give one of the most creative minds in the whole school the special Leonardo da Vinci Prize, for innovative inventions. I believe this young man will go far. Michael Henry, would you step up please?'

Michael's mouth drops open in shock, then his face breaks into the craziest, hugest grin, and I'm just fizzing over with pride bubbles.

I turn to Aunty Lou, and she has a tear in her eye. Michael stumbles over my feet, then runs up the central aisle whooping like he's won the World Cup. Everyone's laughing, especially Miss Petunia, though I can tell she's really trying to put on a serious face as she hands the silver cup, with a red ribbon tied round it, to the mayor, to award to Michael.

Michael beams as the photographer snaps a photo of him shaking the mayor's hand. Michael turns to the audience and bows, and everyone cheers even louder and the year seven boys are chanting, 'Prof M, Prof M, Prof M.'

Mrs Hubert tries to stop them, but they ignore her and, well, she just looks vexed that Michael's won a prize.

Miss Petunia waits for the audience to quieten. Then Felicity Cordour steps forward and says, 'This next prize is the Borough Nature Prize, which I was invited to personally present as it is one close to my heart. I know that you'll be aware of how passionate I am about animal rights.

'The Borough Nature Prize this year goes to a young lady who not only achieves outstanding work in biology, but also saved a frightened, injured fox from the school grounds.'

I hear year sevens whispering to each other, 'It's Nell, Nell's won the prize.' The whisper builds and builds. Aunty Lou's squeezing my arm so hard it hurts, a big smile on her face.

'This young lady bravely stopped some boys from tormenting the poor creature, and sent Michael, our other prize winner, to get Miss Petunia, while she guarded and talked soothingly to the fox. She then phoned the Mr Tod Fox Sanctuary and supervised its rescue. I understand this young lady has quite a collection of rescue animals at home that she loves and cares for. I am told she's the only naturalist on the Beckham Estate. It's my honour to award the Borough Nature Prize to Nell Hobs.'

'Go on, Nell, you go and get your prize, my darling, you deserve it,' says Aunty Lou, kissing me on the cheek.

Everyone starts to cheer and clap as I stand up and walk as slowly as Bob Marley, hoping for a miracle, that my mum'll come in time to see me getting my nature prize. I reach the bottom of the steps that lead to the stage.

'That's my girl.' The voice breaks through the clapping hands. It's Mum! She's come.

Thank you, I say to all the angels in heaven, and I spin round to blow her a kiss.

She waves at me. 'That's my Nelly nell nell,' she shouts a bit too loudly and a few people stop clapping, and turn to stare and no, no, no, no, no, no, not this. Cold trickles up my spine as I see her sway on her feet. Quick as lightening, Aunty Lou is up and whisks her out like a magician.

Though I'm surrounded by cheers, a horror-silence fills my head and I want to disappear right there and then. I wish I could stand on my head so that this pain would go away.

Mr Richardson and all the teachers who are sitting in the front two rows are still clapping. I don't think they even saw. I did, though. I saw. Aunty Lou's empty chair gapes at me. My special moment spoilt.

'Come on, Nell,' calls Miss Petunia, but my legs won't move.

Nell Gwyn takes my hand. 'Hold your head high, ducky, shake your pretty curls and you go up and get that silver cup that you worked so hard for, my darling. It is your just deserts.

So I do, I hold my head high, and I walk up the steps one by one to reach the stage, where Felicity Cordour shakes my hand.

'Well done, Nell,' she says, handing me a big silver cup with a blue ribbon tied around it, and *Nell Hobs* engraved on it. I shake her hand and turn and smile at my audience, even though my heart is shattering into a thousand pieces. Felicity puts her arm round my shoulder, and the camera flashes at me as we pose for the photographs. *Please, Dad, whoever you are, see this picture*, I pray. *I need you*.

I peep at Mr Richardson, to see if he's smiling proudly like a possible dad would, but he isn't even watching me, he is talking to Mrs Hubert. I point my feet and run across the stage and down the steps, clutching my silver cup as daintily as Nell Gwyn would've wished, and then I keep on running down the hall. I need to find Mum. I reach the doors, push them open, straight into Aunty Lou's bear hug.

'I'm so very proud of you,' she whispers into my hair.

Michael appears behind me. 'Whoop whoop, Nell, we're champions!' And he gives me a hug, which he's never ever done before.

More names are called out for prizes in the hall.

'Where's Mum?' I say.

'Let's get you out of here,' says Aunty Lou. Michael and I follow her into the school playground.

'Please, Aunty Lou, where is she?'

'She went off in that direction,' says Aunty Lou, pointing towards the forbidden shortcut.

'I need to find her,' I say, but Aunty Lou grabs hold of me and won't let go.

'No, Nell, no, she is not going to spoil your big moment any more. We're going to walk through the school gates, with our heads held high, because I'm the proudest woman on the planet to have two prize winners to accompany me home.'

So we link arms and march out of the school gate and down the road under the starry sky.

A car beeps behind us – it's Mr Samuels. He winds down the window and sticks his head out.

'Can I give you a lift?' he asks. 'Where do you live?'

'The Beckham Estate, but I wouldn't want to put you out,' says Aunty Lou.

'Oh, that's a coincidence, I'm actually heading there. My mother just moved into number one.'

'That's very kind of you,' says Aunty Lou, as she gets into the seat beside Mr Samuels. Michael and I climb in the back of sir's blue car. Even though there's lots of room, Michael sits really close to me. It feels good to have him near as my bones feel shaky.

'I saw the removal van taking furniture into number one. I've been meaning to knock and welcome our new neighbour to the estate,' says Aunty Lou.

'That's very kind. Mum would love that. I don't know about you but I'm starving,' says Mr Samuels, 'and as we have two prize winners in the car, I feel we should celebrate. How about we go the scenic route?' He turns towards Hampstead, and up a winding lane to a little fish and chip shop tucked into an alcove.

Mr Samuels jumps out of the car and comes back laden with wrapped packages of fish and chips. Then he drives the car further up the road, and parks it in a place where we're looking over the heath.

'This way,' he says and we get out of the car and follow him to a long bench under an oak tree.

'This is where I come to think,' says Mr Samuels.

'It's a beautiful spot for dreams and thoughts,' says Aunty Lou.

We sit in a row on the bench, eating fish and chips, and the salty chips taste so good and start to warm my bones.

'I'm taking my mother on a picnic to Waterlow Park on Sunday,' Mr Samuels tells us, 'to celebrate the start of half term. I was wondering if you would all like to come. I would love her to get to know her neighbours.'

'Oh, pleeeease, Aunty Lou,' whines Michael.

'It doesn't look like you have a choice,' says Mr Samuels with a laugh.

'Very well, we would love to accompany you and your mother on a picnic, as long as you allow me to make the food,' says Aunty Lou.

Mr Samuels smiles and looks a little less faded.

In the distance I can see all the twinkling lights from the windows of rows and rows of houses. I see the Beckham Estate – it looks tiny from up here, like a glittering magical tower. Somewhere behind one of those pretty twinkling lights, in the houses or flats, must be my dad. The thought comforts me. A hedgehog scurries out of a bush next to the bench, and a tawny owl hoots.

Aunty Lou, Mr Samuels and Michael are chatting and laughing.

It's a moment I will remember always, as I clutch my silver cup with my greasy fingers and scoff my chips. I didn't think it was possible to feel so happy and so sad at the same time.

16

As soon as Mr Samuels drives into the courtyard of the Beckham Estate, all the Sunday hopes of picnics, and the memories of warm chips, twinkling lights and laughter vanish.

I scramble out of the car. The kitchen light's on. Mum's home. Buster's outside my front door whining.

Michael and I say our thank yous and good night to Mr Samuels as he walks off towards his mother's flat. Aunty Lou hands Michael her front door key.

'Michael, get TJ ready for *Operation Ark*, I'm going in with Nell.' But then she stops to give him loads more instructions, so I run ahead.

As I get near to my flat I smell burning. Buster starts to howl. I run and look through the kitchen window. A tea towel draped across the cooker's caught fire. My animal family!

'MUM!' I shout. 'MUM!' But she's nowhere to be seen. I ring and ring the bell.

'MUUUUUUUM,' I scream.

Aunty Lou runs up behind me. She bangs on the window yelling, 'STACEY!'

The door opens so suddenly I fall through it, still clutching my silver cup.

Mum's standing there shivering in her bath robe, hair dripping wet, clutching a cup of coffee.

I push past her and run into the kitchen, followed by Aunty Lou and Buster. I fill a pan with water, and throw it over the burning tea towel.

'Well done, Nell,' says Aunty Lou, opening a window. There are soot marks up the kitchen wall.

'Mum, the whole flat could've set fire, you could've killed my animal family. You could've set fire to Aunty Lou's.'

But my shouting's upsetting Buster, he has a bit of my school trousers in his teeth and he's tugging, wanting me out of the kitchen.

'It's OK, boy,' I say. 'The fire's out.'

But I can still smell burning.

Grabbing an oven glove, I open the oven door, and I take out a baking tray, with burnt-to-a-cinder little charcoal sticks on it.

'I'm sorry,' says Mum. 'I forgot about them. I was just trying to cook you some oven chips. I thought you might be hungry after your—'

'I don't want chips,' I say, sobbing. 'I've had chips. I just wanted you to see me getting my prize, without making a show of yourself. Is that too much to ask?'

Mum's face crumples.

'Nell,' she says, 'well done for getting a prize,' and she goes to hug me. On her breath I can smell drink mixed with the coffee she drinks to sober herself up. I shake her off.

'What prize did I get? Can you even remember?'

'You got, erm . . . a prize for good school work.'

'No, Mum, I didn't, 'cause my school work isn't good, not really. In fact, no word of a lie, it's rubbish. Most probably 'cause I can't concentrate, 'cause I'm so worried about you all the time. I got the Borough Nature Prize, IF YOU'RE INTERESTED!'

'Isn't my Nelly nell nell clever getting the nature prize,' Mum says to Aunty Lou, who's putting the blackened remains of the tea towel and oven chips in the bin. 'She loves her Bob Marley and her Asbo and Chaos and her whatsername goldfish.'

'It was my special day, Mum, the most special

moment in my whole life, and I've been hugging the secret inside me for weeks, dreaming of making you proud.'

Mum holds her arms out to me. 'Nell, I love you. I try I really do try but—'

'Trying's not good enough, Mum, not any more.'

'Nell, go and get your animals ready. I need to talk to your mum,' says Aunty Lou.

I close the kitchen door behind me but stay and listen, ear squashed against the wood, 'cause this is me they're talking about and I've got to know what's being said.

'Stacey, it was nearly game over this evening. If I hadn't got you out of there, if the teachers had seen . . . ! The only reason that I don't report you to children's services is 'cause she loves you and those animals more than life itself, and it would destroy that little girl to be parted from any of you, but this can't go on.'

I shiver hearing the words *this can't go on* spoken aloud.

'You've done so brilliantly these last few weeks. What went wrong tonight?'

'I got scared,' says Mum. 'Scared that I was going to let my Nell down and that I wouldn't know what to say to the teachers, so I thought I'd just have the one . . .'

'You've got to step up, Stacey, and be a mum, and you haven't got long. Nell will be a woman soon enough.'

I look down at my lady bumps, still flat as a pancake. Being a woman seems a long way off. It's the here and now that needs sorting out.

Then Mum starts to cry, and I try but I can't hear what Aunty Lou's saying.

I go to my bedroom, followed by Buster, who keeps nudging my leg with his nose.

My lead legs are too heavy to even stand on my head. I curl into a ball and shut my eyes, cuddling Buster.

I am sinking down, down, down, *the whole of London is on fire. Rows of wooden houses, burning down. I hear horses' hooves getting nearer, as I crouch down in a doorway of a house the fire has not yet reached.*

Carts rattle past me, piled high with people's worldly possessions, trying to get away from the Great Fire of London. Children cry, a women screams. Then a cart passes, piled high with my scatter cushions and my favourite turquoise one falls off the cart, into a muddy puddle, and gets trampled on by the men, women and children, all trying to escape the fire. Then I hear them, Asbo and Chaos are calling to me. My animal family are on the cart and they are getting further away from me, and I reach and reach for them but the crowds and the heat from the fire are stopping me. I look down at my feet. Bob Marley is traipsing along next to me with my lost Noah's ark charm bracelet balanced on his shell. He was too slow, too slow to get on the cart. It's just Bob Marley and me. The rest of my life has vanished.

My nostrils fill with the smell of oranges and I hear my name being called. King Charles II is riding through the streets, ordering houses to be blown up so that the fire can't reach across the gaps. Then Nell Gwyn appears behind me and takes me in her arms.

I wake with a start and wander through to the kitchen.

Mum's bedroom door's still closed and I hear Aunty Lou's and Mum's murmuring voices.

I fill a bucket from under the sink and a scrubbing brush and start scrubbing the soot from the wall. I wonder if King Charles II helped people clean their kitchens after the Great Fire of London.

As I scrub and scrub, I just keep thinking that if only I had a dad this wouldn't have happened.

17

Aunty Lou and I spent all of Saturday making food for our picnic. By Saturday evening, Mum has sobered up and promised to never ever drink again. Again.

'It was a temporary blip, Nell,' she says. Like I haven't heard that one before! The sun shines through my window on picnic day, making the water in Beyoncé and Destiny's tank sparkle.

I feed my animal family, shower, drag on my on my jeans and orange T-shirt that says *Nature Rocks* at world champion breakneck speed, and grab my rucksack.

'Mum,' I call, pushing open her door, but she's on her back snoring. 'Mum, get up, you've got to get ready for our picnic.'

'All right,' mumbles Mum, 'leave me to wake up, can't you?'

I put a few empty jam jars in my school rucksack in case I find any insects that need rescuing, leave the door on the latch and run next door to Aunty Lou's. I hear TJ and Michael shouting at each other before Aunty Lou even opens the door.

Michael has on a yellow spotted shirt and a red bow tie. He's clutching his briefcase.

'Can't you ever look normal? Mum, tell him,' says TJ. 'I bought you trainers, I bought you hoodies. I even bought you T-shirts out of my own money. Why, Michael? WHY CAN'T YOU JUST DRESS LIKE A NORMAL BOY?'

Aunty Lou pulls me inside. 'TJ, stop shouting please, NOW. Michael has the right to dress and express himself however he wants to.'

Michael grins. 'I'm dressed in these fine clothes 'cause I'm going on a picnic with sir, and I want to look smart. Now, would you all come this way please.'

We follow him into his bedroom. The shelf with the railway track goes right the way round his room now, and on it is a brilliant miniature stream train. The engine is made of red painted wood, with *Ark Express* painted on the side in gold. Behind it are the carriages, which are made of those plastic tubs that washing machine capsules come in, sitting on what looks like old roller skate wheels. On the side of each carriage, my animal family names – Fiz and Tyrone, Aunty Lou, Asbo and Chaos, Beyoncé and Destiny and Bob Marley – are painted.

Michael fishes out sparkling new food dishes from his briefcase, each with one of my animal family's names painted on the side.

'Nell, if you could assist me, and dot these round the room, under the track.'

I quickly do what he asks.

'You've got a dish for the fish,' I say, holding up a tiny dish with *Beyoncé and Destiny* painted on the side. 'Fishes don't eat from dishes.'

'You'll see, Nell,' he says, tapping the side of his nose. 'Behold,' he announces, waving a remote control with a flourish.

'That's the missing remote control from the TV in my room!' shouts TJ. 'I'VE BEEN LOOKING FOR THAT FOR MONTHS!'

'TJ, hush your mouth and let Michael finish,' says Aunty Lou.

'Behold,' says Michael again. He presses a button on the remote control and the train starts to move slowly along the track.

'The *Ark Express* is specially designed to deliver the right quantity of food for Nell's animal family. Even Beyoncé and Destiny will have a tiny quantity of fish food tipped into the dish, ready for you, Nell, to sprinkle into their fish bowl. For the purpose of this demonstration, ladies and gentleman, I have just put some guinea pig pellets in Asbo and Chaos's carriage and some chopped lettuce in Bob Marley's carriage.'

Michael presses the remote and the train stops when Bob Marley's carriage is aligned with the dish underneath. He presses another button and the carriage slowly tips over, revealing a yellow shoelace that ties it to the next carriage. The chopped-up lettuce starts to fall into the dish underneath.

TJ catapults forwards. 'That's my trainer lace, all these carriages are held together with my new trainer laces.'

The train makes a strange creaking noise, and the whole thing tips over, flinging guinea pig pellets and bits of lettuce in TJ's face. A bit of wet lettuce sticks to the end of his nose.

We all gasp, then Aunty Lou starts laughing, tears pouring down her cheeks, and Michael's rolling on the floor holding his belly, and I can't stop the giggles exploding out of me, even though TJ looks vexed.

'How am I even related to you, Michael? How, how, how?' says TJ, brushing himself down. He runs out of the room and comes back moments later with his arms full of trainers with no laces.

He looks so cross that we just laugh harder, then he starts to laugh too as he brushes himself down.

'Michael, the Ark Express is, no word of a lie, the most brilliant invention ever.'

'It will be,' says Michael, 'one of my finest once I perfect a few details.'

A car horn hoots. I open the front door and there's sir, helping his mother and her cute little black and tan Cavalier King Charles spaniel into the car. He climbs into the front and waves to us.

'Aunty Lou, sir's here.' I walk to the kitchen where Aunty Lou's packing a huge picnic hamper basket with silver-foil-wrapped food. I smell the fried chicken and potato salad – my favourites – that we cooked and prepared yesterday.

Aunty Lou's dressed up in a red flowery dress and red ballet pump shoes.

'You look lovely, Aunty Lou,' I say, giving her a hug. 'I've told Mum to get dressed.'

Aunty Lou raises her eyes to the sky. 'I'll go and hurry her up,' she says.

I pack the last few silver-foil-wrapped packages.

Michael and I take one handle each of the heavy hamper, and walk out to the car.

'Good morning, sir,' Michael and I chorus.

Sir's mum's Cavalier is barking.

Aunty Lou marches out of my front door, pulling it to on the latch. I can see the anger bristles sparking off her.

'Your mother prefers to sleep than come on our picnic,' she says. 'But, Nell, it's fine, we're going to have a lovely time without her.' She climbs into the front seat of the car.

If I'm really honest with myself, I'm a teensy wincey bit relieved Mum's not coming, so I don't have to constantly watch out for her. But no sooner have I had this thought than guilt floods me.

It's as if Aunty Lou reads my thoughts. She's looking at me and she says, 'We all need our own space sometimes. Good morning, Mr Samuels.'

'Please call me Daniel, we're not at school now.'

'Your name's Daniel Samuels,' I say, a giggle escaping before I can trap it.

'My mother's idea of a joke,' says Mr Samuels.

In the car we meet Mr Samuels' mother, Mary, and her Cavalier spaniel, Tutty.

'Can I stroke Tutty please?'

Mary nods, and I reach out and I let the little dog sniff my hand, to introduce myself, and then I stroke his soft, black head and long, silky ears. I just love Waterlow Park and the house that stands in it, Lauderdale House. I used to come up here when I was little and have the best of times in the art workshops they held here on the magical days when Mum's drink demon hadn't captured her. I haven't been up to the park for ages.

We find a lovely spot on the lawn. Aunty Lou lays a rug down and Michael and I help her set out the delicious picnic as Tutty tears round and round, barking and rolling and sniffing, and nearly tripping everyone up.

'Keep Tutty away from the picnic!' shouts Aunty Lou. I catch the little dog and give him a cuddle.

Our picnic is a feast: fried chicken and jerk chicken and potato salad and coleslaw and crisps and fried snappers and those tiny tomatoes and salad and cupcakes and strawberries and chocolate cake and mango juice to drink. It's just the best feast in the world.

Aunty Lou and Mr Samuels sit on garden chairs and Mary sits in her wheelchair. Michael and I plonk ourselves on the rug. We all fill our plates with food, but I help Mary first and she smiles a twinkly smile as I hand her a plate.

'Well, Daniel,' says Aunty Lou, 'the children say that your history lessons are very lively, and if you can keep these two engaged, you must have such a gift for teaching.'

'My son has a passion for the history,' says Mary.

'I belong to a reenactment society,' says Mr Samuels. 'We meet and act out the historic battles between the Roundheads and Cavaliers,' and he talks to Aunty Lou about the Battle of Naseby, while I stuff my face with fried chicken and coleslaw and crisps.

'But of course, Lou, you know about this already, as we're going to reenact the battle on the wasteland, followed by a pageant, in which of course Michael is to be King Charles II and Nell will be Nell Gwyn.'

I nearly choke as I hear the word *pageant*. I'm suddenly not hungry any more.

'What!' says Aunty Lou. 'Why didn't I know about this?

'I tried to tell you at parents' evening,' says Mr

Samuels. 'But I gave Michael a letter to take home to you.'

Aunty Lou grabs Michael's briefcase, and tips it upside down. Cogs and springs and strange-looking unidentifiable objects go rolling around on the grass. I scoop up Tutty, as he think the cogs and springs are toys. A screwed-up piece of paper lands next to the crisps.

Aunty Lou smooths it out and reads the letter. 'Michael! Why didn't you tell me?'

'I forgot,' mumbles Michael.

'Michael, you are to play the king of England and you FORGET TO TELL YOUR AUNTY?'

'And you, Nell, why didn't you tell me?'

Misery fills my bones as I delve into my rucksack and pull out the greasy, dirty, gold material, still with bits of sawdust stuck to it. I blink hard to stop my eyes leaking in front of Mr Samuels.

'I've been trying to make a Nell Gwyn costume, but it's gone all wrong.'

'Nell, why didn't you say anything?'

''Cause Mum promised she would help me,' I say.

'Oh, Nell,' says Aunty Lou, 'this is easily fixed,' and she presses a speed dial on her mobile and starts talking to Gracie, her best friend.

'That's sorted then, we're having an emergency costume-making session this evening. Daniel, I promise you these two will be dressed in costumes that do your history pageant proud.'

'I look forward very much to seeing Nell and Michael dressed in all their finery,' says Mr Samuels, pouring us all another glass of mango juice. Aunty Lou and sir clink glasses and smile at each other.

Michael is stuffing the bits for his inventions back into his briefcase. Aunty Lou cuts the yummy, gooey chocolate cake and I help her put it on plates and give it out to everyone. I eat my cake sitting cross-legged, looking at Lauderdale House. Mary leans forward and grabs my wrist.

''Twas her house, you know. Nell Gwyn's, the king rented it for her as a summer house.'

I couldn't believe it.

'It's true,' says Mr Samuels, 'and she held her son out of that window by his ankles and she said, "Unless you give my son a title I shall drop him," and the king said, "Save the Earl of Burford."'

I stare up at the window he pointed to. All those times I had done art workshops at Lauderdale House and I never knew that. I wonder if the king had done colouring with his children. I bet King

Charles II was good at colouring.

Tutty climbs on my knee.

Mary's watching me.

'He's called after her dog, you know.'

'Whose dog?' I ask.

'Nell Gwyn's, she had a toy spaniel called Tutty. Don't think I don't know what goes on in that school of yours. I make my son tell me everything.'

Nell Gwyn loved dogs like I do! She really was a naturalist.

'King Charles adored his toy spaniels,' says Mary. 'Today's King Charles and Cavalier King Charles are their descendants, so they are.'

Tutty licks my hand. So Mary's dog Tutty had dog relatives going back and back in time, that would've known Nell Gwyn and the king. Nell Gwyn would've given Tutty's ancestor a cuddle. I feel fluttery in my heart at the very thought.

Mary winks at me. I've sat still for too long – I need to stretch my legs. I run down the sloping lawn with Tutty scampering beside me, down the steps with the stone eagles either side. I swirl around the oak, ash and sycamore trees, reaching out to touch the rough bark. I spin faster and faster, I hear laughter and *there before me is Nell Gwyn, in a yellow dress, hiding behind a tree, playing hide-and-seek with the king, who's counting to one hundred.*

'I am coming to find you,' he calls.

Nell puts her finger to her lips. 'Ssh,' she whispers, 'don't let him find us.'

Then an arm reaches out and grabs her wrist. Nell Gwyn squeals.

'I've got you,' says the king but Nell Gwyn wriggles away and runs down to the lake. I run after them, Tutty barking, enjoying the fun. The king chases Nell round the lake and catches her and gives her a kiss. Then King Charles scoops up Tutty and hands the little dog to Nell Gwyn, who kisses him on his head, and puts him on the grass to play. Then they vanish in the spring breeze.

I walk back to the picnic.

Mary grabs my arm and her deep blue eyes spark into mine. 'You see them, don't you, the king and Nell?'

'How do you know?' I whisper.

'Old Mary knows everything,' she says, chuckling.

I run across the grass to Lauderdale House, and open the door and peer through. There are lots of old people looking at paintings. I dodge past them and up the staircase. There's a lovely long yellow room. It is completely empty.

I hold my arms out, twirl around and dance a jig down the room. There is an old beam in the wall, preserved just as it would've been when Nell Gwyn lived here. I place my palm flat on it and my touch splinters back through time.

Nell swirls past me, dancing, twirling a little giggling boy of about three years old.

Round and round they go, faster and faster. King Charles II stands in the doorway, clapping. He winks at me as he laughs. Nell sees the king and, letting go of the little boy, she runs down the room and jumps into the king's arms. He gives her a kiss on the cheek.

'Hello, my Nelly nell nell,' he says.

Nell squirms out of his arms, runs to the window and opens it.

'Wave to me, Nelly, as I walk,' says the king.

Nell Gwyn and I look out of the window, till we can see King Charles below.

She grabs her son by the ankles. He's laughing, thinking it is the best game ever invented, as she dangles him out of the window.

'Unless you give my son a title I shall drop him,' Nell Gwyn shouts down to the king.

'Save the Earl of Burford!' shouts King Charles, *rushing forward to catch him should he be dropped, properly claiming the little boy as his own. Nell Gwyn hauls the little boy back into the room, hugging him to her. 'You're my little Earl of Burford,' she says, kissing him, then smiles down at the king as they vanish into the mist of time.*

I peep out of the window. Aunty Lou, sir, Mary and Michael smile and wave up at me. If I was held upside down out of the window, would my dad come forward?

'Will you catch me, Dad, whoever you are?' I whisper. Would he even care enough to? I feel a breeze on my neck and what sounds like a little kid chuckling. I turn around but no one's there.

I can see Aunty Lou handing out more slices of chocolate cake. I need to get back to the picnic before Michael scoffs the lot.

I run to the top of the stairs, jumping down them two at a time, dodging the old people looking at paintings. I make it to the door.

I run across the grass and, plonking myself next to Michael, grab the last slice of yummy cake. Mr Samuels is playing with Tutty so we can eat our cake in peace. Chocolate cake's not good for dogs. I know this being a naturalist. A tired-looking bee lands on my chocolatey finger.

'Keep very still, Nell,' says Aunty Lou.

'I'm not scared,' I say but I do keep really still and, with my other hand, I grab hold of one of the jam jars in my rucksack. Then I stick my finger with the bee slowly, slowly into it. The bee flies off my finger up into the jar, and quickly I grab my picnic plate, put it over the mouth of the jam jar and carefully stand up and walk over to a white rose bush, and let the bee fly on to it, so that it can suckle nectar, which will be better for the bee than cake.

It has been the perfect picnic.

Gracie opens the door of her flat on the eighteenth floor, to let Michael, Aunty Lou and me into her kitchen.

And there's Sasha sitting at the table, next to the sewing machine, sorting through piles of material. She turns to me and smiles and my cheeks burn as I smile back.

'Come in, make yourselves at home. We've been hard at work ever since you phoned, Lou,' says Gracie.

I pull the library book out of my rucksack and find the picture of Nell Gwyn.

'I've got to look like this,' I say.

'You will do, by the time I've finished with you,' says Sasha.

'Show them that wig you've ordered for Michael, on that phone of yours,' says Gracie, who's putting the kettle on.

Sasha holds out her phone to show us the long black curly wig. Michael starts strutting round the room with a puffed-out chest.

'Odds fish! I'm the king, Nell, you gotta do what I tell you.'

'You'll be lucky. No word of a lie, Michael, that's never going to happen,' I say.

'No, Michael,' says Aunty Lou, 'I think you'll find *you've* got to do what *I* tell you.'

And she makes him stand on a chair as she measures him, which is a difficult task. 'Will you stand still?' she says.

I pull out the sorry lump of gold material that is meant to be my costume.

'Mum gave me this,' I say to Gracie, 'she said she'd help me . . .'

Gracie prises it from my fist and puts her arm round me. 'Shall we give it a wash and start again?'

I nod. 'It got ripped at school,' I mutter.

'Nell, we'll soon sort that, don't you worry,' says Gracie.

Sasha takes my hand. 'Come this way,' she says and she leads me towards Gracie's bedroom. On the door is a glittery yellow star and underneath is a sign that says *Nell Hobs*.

'Your dressing room awaits, Miss Nell,' she says, pushing open the door.

There are costumes everywhere hanging on metal clothes-rails on wheels. I feel like I'm in a dream as I run my hands along the velvets, silks and lace in a rainbow of gold, deep purples, reds, silvers, all the colours that you could possibly think of.

'They're part of the collection of vintage clothes my mum left me, there's bound to be something we can use,' says Sasha.

'Thank you for your kindness, Sasha,' I say.

'Nell, you're doing me a proper favour. I leapt at the chance when Gracie told me. I've got to do a costume project on Restoration theatre, as part of my performing arts course – that's the time of Nell Gwyn. Will you be my model? I've got to take some photos for the project.'

'Me a model? Course!' I say, excitement bubbling inside me.

'I think it's so cool that you're going to be Nell Gwyn in the costume pageant,' says Sasha. 'If it weren't for Nell Gwyn, I wouldn't be at performing arts college at all. She was one of the first actresses. Before that it was men playing women's parts.'

'Really?' I say. 'That's special.'

'Yes,' says Sasha, 'we're learning about those early actresses in college. The plays were at three o'clock in the afternoon, when it was still light, as they had no electricity then.'

'Like us when Mum hasn't got money for the meter key,' I say.

Sasha hugs me.

'Mr Samuels told us that Nell Gwyn was only fourteen when she acted in her first play as a professional actress,' I say.

'That's proper incredible, if you ask me,' says Sasha, 'and they would do about fifty different plays a season. She couldn't read or write, so I'd love to know how she learned her lines, and she must've been brilliant, 'cause Dryden the playwright wrote comic parts especially for her.'

I drink in these details of Nell Gwyn, my honorary ancestor, storing them in my brain for ever.

'Did your mum work in the theatre?' I ask.

Sasha rummages through her bag, pulling out a photograph of a lady who looks a tiny bit like Sasha, only she has bleached blonde spiky hair. She's sitting on a big trunk that has *Zebra Blue On Tour* plastered across it. She is looking into the eyes of Fox, Sasha's dad, when he was young and good-looking. The photo's filled with love.

'Yes, she started off working in theatre but then she did the costumes for my dad's band Zebra Blue. That photo was taken before she left us,' says Sasha.

'Oh,' I say. All my words running away from me.

'The thing is, Nell, you and I have both had to bring ourselves up. My dad tried, but he even used to forget to tell me that I had to go to school.'

I laugh. I love it that Sasha understands.

'My mum left and took all her chaos with her,' went on Sasha, 'but you, my little Nell, have to live with it day in day out, and I think you're one amazing young girl, with the troubles of a grown woman on your shoulders. I have proper respect for you and if ever you need to talk . . .'

I look into her eyes, and I sink on to the end of Gracie's bed, feeling the cold silk quilt through my jeans, but I can't let any words out of my mouth, 'cause if I let them spill out, my words will fill the whole of the Beckham Estate, and we'll all drown in them. But the fact that she cares, that she understands, means everything.

'Let's have some proper fun,' says Sasha, squeezing the top of my arm.

Sasha picks out a pair of white bloomers and a little corset top from the clothes on the rail.

'Put these on,' she says. 'The long bloomers will be good to wear underneath if the wind blows your skirt up.'

I feel a little shy as I scrabble out of my jeans. The corset top and bloomers actually fit me.

'I don't have any lady bumps,' I say, looking down at my flat chest.

'You will,' says Sasha, smiling, as she finds a huge yellow silk petticoat, which she lifts over the top of my head and wriggles down to my waist. No word of a lie, it's perfect, but it's way too long.

'Gracie can take that up,' says Sasha.

The costumes are getting flung everywhere as Sasha burrows through them.

'Ah, this is what I'm looking for.' And she puts it over my head. It's a white blouse with huge puffy sleeves and a white lace collar.

'See, what I'm thinking,' says Sasha, 'is we can

make your gold material that your mum gave you into a dress to go over the top of this.'

I nod, excitement in my belly. I'm going to have a costume. Sasha swoops down and picks up an old curtain of beautiful red and gold embroidered flowers.

'We can decorate it with this.'

Sasha leads me to her dressing table. I sit on the pink silk cushioned chair. Sasha picks up a brush and fluffs out my curls.

'There we go! See, you'll be the image of Nell Gwyn.'

I smile at Sasha in the mirror. 'I reckon Nell Gwyn could handle herself,' I say. 'She wouldn't let anyone put her down.'

'And you mustn't let anyone put you down, Nell Hobs, 'cause you are proper amazing,' says Sasha.

I stand up and I fling my arms around her, and she holds me tight for the longest time.

'Let's go and show them next door.'

Michael is still standing on the chair.

'WILL YOU STAND STILL?' shouts Aunty Lou, who's pinning up some brown velvet breeches. Gracie is at her machine sewing ruffs on to a shirt.

They turn to look at me.

Aunty Lou claps her hands. 'Oh, my Nell, you look as pretty as a picture . . .'

'You've done a good job, Sasha,' says Gracie. 'You've inherited your mum's talent.'

'You look good, Nell,' says Michael.

'Why so do you, Your Majesty,' I say, curtsying to him.

'Odds fish, we are going to be the best dressed people in the costume parade,' says Michael and we link thumbs.

Michael and I spend the rest of the evening being prodded and poked and pinned and finally my gold material, which has been drying on the radiator, is added to my costume and decorated with the gold and red curtain material, with a panel at the front and trims on the sleeves. It's perfect!

Aunty Lou disappears and I hear a yapping when she returns. She has Tutty in her arms.

'I thought for the photographs . . .' says Aunty Lou.

Mary has kindly lent us him and, no word of a lie, I have the most fun being a model, holding little Tutty, as Sasha and Aunty Lou take photos of me and Tutty and Michael.

'Do you want to go and show your mum?' says Aunty Lou.

I nod. 'I don't know how to thank you all, honest, I don't,' I say, giving Aunty Lou, Gracie and Sasha a kiss. I bundle my jeans and T-shirt into my school rucksack and, holding up my skirt so it won't get dirty, I travel down in the lift to the ground floor and knock on the door of my flat.

Mum opens the door, dressed in jeans and a red jumper. She smiles. 'Oh my! You do look the part. The perfect Nell Gwyn.'

I feel chuffed as I parade round the front room for Mum.

'How did you get the costume?' she asks.

'Aunty Lou, of course. She arranged everything. These are from Sasha,' I say, showing her the bloomers and the yellow silk petticoat and corset underneath the gold dress, 'and Gracie made this over-dress with your gold bridesmaid material, and she did the decorations.' I try to bite my words but they don't stop. 'But it was meant to be you, Mum, just you and me together. You promised to make me a costume, but you lied.'

Mum's face turns as pale as milk.

'I'm so sorry,' she says and reaches out to me.

I push past her and run into my bedroom, slamming the door.

I don't put the light on. I stand in the middle of my bedroom with wobbly legs. *Nell Gwyn steps out of the shadows and curtsys to me.*

'Good night, my little Nell Hobs,' she says.

'Good night, Nell Gwyn,' I say and curtsy back.

Mum bangs on the door. 'Let me in, Nell, please. I'm so sorry. I promise to do better.'

But I've heard it all before.

'Go away,' I say, and I feed my animal family and change into my PJs. I stand on my head till the sting of my words with Mum goes from my heart. Then I snuggle under the covers, cuddling my turquoise scatter cushion.

'*Sleep tight, Nell Gwyn,*' I whisper into the shadows.

18

My shoulder is being gently shaken.

'Nell, wake up.' It's Mum.

I turn over and shut my eyes, ignoring her.

She shakes my shoulder again.

'Come on, Nell. *Ride a cock-horse to Banbury Cross, to see a fine lady upon a white horse. Rings on her fingers and bells on her toes, she shall have music wherever she goes.*'

She keeps saying it over and over again until I giggle, the sting from last night's row vanishing.

'Get dressed. We're going on an outing.'

'Where, Mum?' I say, sitting bolt upright in bed. Outings are special things. We hardly ever go on outings since Mum's demon came to live with us.

'What's the time, Mum?'

'It's five o'clock in the morning.'

'It's a bit early to be going out, isn't it?'

'You'll see,' she says, tapping the end of my nose.

Mum feeds my animal family while I get dressed quick as I can. We grab our matching summer khaki parkas and go out into the dark courtyard of the Beckham Estate.

As Mum locks the door, I plead, 'Please, Mum, where are we going?'

'It's a secret, just you and me together for ever.'

She grabs my hand as we walk across the courtyard, to the Patels' newsagent.

Mrs Patel is sorting out the newspapers and smiles as we come in.

'You're up bright and early. Where are you going on this fresh spring morning?'

'It's a secret,' says Mum. 'I'm taking Nell on a surprise half-term treat.' And she puts money on our Oyster cards and buys croissants, a jar of Nutella, bananas, a chocolate milkshake for me and a strawberry one for her. She also buys a bunch of white roses.

Mrs Patel squeezes Mum's arm. 'Have a lovely, lovely time with your daughter. Times spent together are precious, remember that, Stacey.'

'Remember that,' she repeats, as we leave the shop.

We walk to the bus stop and Mum holds my hand like I'm a little kid, but I don't mind. Mum cuddles me as we wait for the bus. I'm lost in her warmth and honeysuckle perfume. Hopping up the stairs, we snuggle in our parkas, on the back row of the empty bus, like a couple of naughty school kids.

Mum is looking at maps and reading information on her mobile phone. I sneak a peek, but she snatches it from my gaze. I look out of the window as the bus winds its way through sleeping Camden Town, then on its way to Oxford Street, and I watch as London begins to open its eyes, ready for the day. Finally, we reach Victoria.

Mum pulls me off the bus and grabs my hand as we cross the road, and walk through a black gate into St James's Park.

I see a half full wine bottle sticking out of a bin. I run over and cover it with a paper bag that I snatch up as it's blowing along the path.

'Nell, leave that,' calls Mum. I turn and see her looking at me, sadness in her eyes.

'Come here,' she says, pulling me over to the kids' play area.

We sit on the swings, seeing who can go the highest. Mum's hair blows in the breeze, like a golden cobweb. She jumps off, pulling me with her as we run along the path.

'Now for breakfast,' says Mum and we sit near a willow tree, as the geese and coots and ducks crowd round us. My most favourite birds are mallard ducks – the baby duck will ride on its mother's back while she's swimming. I wish I was a baby duck, then Mum might not leave me. Not ever.

We dip our croissants and bits of banana into the Nutella and guzzle our milkshakes. A mist shimmers of the lake, and it's our most perfect time ever.

'Follow me,' says Mum, and we walk across a patterned bridge. The geese waddle in front of our feet, nearly tripping us up.

Then out of the park we go, crossing the road until we're standing in front of St James's Palace.

'This is one of the palaces where King Charles II lived,' says Mum.

I shut my eyes, and the King Charles dad daydream takes over. *My whole class come round to tea. I ring a bell and Mrs Hubert and Chantal Smith, dressed in maid's uniforms, come running and curtsy to me.*

'It is time for our banquet,' I order.

'What are you daydreaming about?' asks Mum.

'Nothing,' I lie.

'Come with me,' she says, and round the corner we go.

'Look,' says Mum.

We're standing outside a big house. And there on the wall of the house is a blue plaque. It says: *Nell Gwyn lived in a house on this site from 1671–1687.* No word of a lie. Nell Gwyn, my honorary ancestor, lived on this very spot.

'I thought you might like to leave a flower for her,' says Mum, and I pick one of the white roses from the bunch and lay it on the pavement, outside the house, on the spot where Nell Gwyn once lived.

Mum takes a selfie of us with the blue Nell Gwyn plaque in the background. Then on we go, towards Trafalgar Square.

'Come on,' she says. 'Time for the next bit of our magical mystery tour,' and I follow Mum round the corner to the National Portrait Gallery.

'This way,' says Mum. 'We've got to find room seven.'

We ride up the longest of all escalators, walk round a corner and there she is: Nell Gwyn on the wall, next to a painting of King Charles, who's looking a bit grumpy, if you ask me. Nell Gwyn looks wise, as if she has the secrets of the world at her fingertips.

I sit on the wooden bench and drink the pictures into my brain, so they will stay there for ever and ever. Chantal Smith doesn't have paintings of her honorary ancestor in a gallery!

I wonder if my dad has long black curly hair, like King Charles's wig. I look at Mum, and the words *Mum please tell me about my dad* are balanced on the end of my tongue, but I swallow them, 'cause I cannot risk stressing her out.

I take a white rose and put it under Nell Gwyn's portrait. A lady in a red coat smiles.

'That's a pretty flower,' she says.

'Nell Gwyn's my honorary ancestor,' I say. 'Just being respectful.'

'Come,' says Mum, and we take the lift right to the top of the building and walk into a café with a view over the rooftops of London. We sit and look at Big Ben, the Houses of Parliament and the London Eye, as we drink our hot chocolate with mountains of cream on the top.

Mum's got a blob on the end of her nose. I snatch her phone and take a photo before she can stop me. Mum dips her finger in the cream on top of her hot chocolate, and dabs the end of my nose. A man on the next table rustles his newspaper and glares daggers at us. Mum sticks her tongue out at him.

'Really!' he says, and Mum and I start proper belly laughing.

'We better get out of here before we are thrown out,' says Mum, and she pays the bill and we leave.

'On to the next bit of our magical mystery tour,' says Mum and we cut through the streets, till we're standing outside the Theatre Royal Drury Lane.

'This stands on the spot of the very Kings Theatre where Nell Gwyn acted in plays,' says Mum, reading from her phone.

I point my feet as best I can in my trainers and dance a jig. Mum is clapping; a policeman walks past and laughs. I curtsy to him and snatch a white rose, grab Mum's hand and follow the building round, till we're at stage door, and I place the white rose on the pavement outside.

'We're going to find where Nell Gwyn was born,' says Mum.

'Sir said it was the top end of Drury Lane,' I say, remembering my first magical history class with Mr Samuels.

So we walk up to the top of Drury Lane, to

Stuckley Street, reading information from Wikipedia as we go.

'This is where she was born. Cole Yard Alley once stood here,' says Mum.

My breath catches in the back of my throat. I wonder if Nell Gwyn ever walked slowly, slowly home, scared what state her mum would be in when she got there.

I lay a white rose when I reach the spot, and we walk down to the bottom of Drury Lane, scattering white petals as we go, down to where the Cock and Pie pub once stood, where it is said Nell Gwyn had her lodgings when she worked as an actress.

I close my eyes.

'I am late, so late for the theatre,' says Nell Gwyn with a giggle. A breeze ripples through me and her lips brush my cheek as she rushes past, holding her skirts above her ankles, as she runs down muddy Drury Lane.

Mum takes my hand, and we walk back to Trafalgar Square and into St-Martin-in-the-Fields church, where we finish up our magical mystery tour.

'Nell Gwyn's buried under the altar of the St-Martin-in-the-Fields church, which stood here then,' says Mum, and we light a candle and say a prayer, and I walk up to the altar by myself and leave another white rose.

'Thank you for looking over me, Nell Gwyn,' I say. 'Thank you for understanding. Thank you, most of all, for giving me this day with my mum.'

I walk back to Mum, past a homeless man asleep on the pew.

'Did you like your magical mystery tour?' says Mum.

'It's perfect, a golden day,' I say, flinging my arms around her, pricking my hand on the thorn of the one white rose that Mum's still clutching.

We spend the afternoon in Covent Garden, watching street entertainers juggling fire, standing on their heads, and singing high notes that shatter glass. My feet throb, but I don't care; I'm with my mum, and I'm holding, with all my strength, on to every single perfect second, while we're in our love bubble that keeps us safe from the rest of the world.

'I'm busting for a wee,' says Mum, 'there's bound to be a pub somewhere.'

The bubble bursts.

'No, Mum, please no. Maybe one of the theatres will let us use their toilets?'

Mum gives me a funny look. 'I only want to go to the loo, Nell, honestly, what a fuss.'

I'm now desperate for a wee too, and I'm searching for anywhere we might be able to go to the toilet that doesn't serve alcohol. We come to a pub called the White Swan but it has a separate black and white tiled entrance to reach the toilets upstairs. It's divided from the bar area by a wall of windows, through which I can see lots of people drinking.

I don't think I can hold on much longer without wetting myself. Perhaps if we run up the stairs and straight back down after we've used the toilets Mum won't be tempted.

'Race you,' I say, and Mum runs up the stairs ahead of me, laughing. I deliberately lose the race so I'm behind her, to make sure she goes into the toilet.

I can smell beer in the air.

Mum and I race into cubicles. I wee as quick as I can, but Mum's quicker, and pulls her chain. I hear her wash her hands.

'I'll just be outside the door,' she calls, as I hear it swing shut behind her. I pull my chain.

'Please wait for me,' I call, and run out to wash my hands, not stopping to dry them.

I open the door but there's no one there.

'Mum,' I call, 'Mum?' I rush back into the loo, in case she's gone back into the toilets, but they're all empty. The last remaining white rose lies balanced on the sink. I snatch it up, rush down the stairs, and look through the wall of windows. The pub's packed but I make out a toss of blonde hair. Mum's in the corner with a drink in her hand. Sadness, disgust, disappointment and anger hit my heart – bang, bang, bang. Couldn't she make it special for me even for just one day?

Then all of a sudden a crowd of men rise, singing that song 'He's getting married in the morning', taking Mum twirling and staggering around with them.

'MUM!' I scream, trying to reach her, but I can't get to her – the street outside is jam-packed with people on their way to the theatres.

''Scuse me,' I say. 'Sorry. I need to get to my mum.' And as I try to push past, a lady in a light blue coat, her arm round her daughter and theatre tickets clutched in her hand says, 'Ah, you all right, love?'

I shake my head and dive back through the door of the White Swan pub, and halfway up the stairs that lead to the toilets. I sink down on a step and I wait and I wait but Mum doesn't come back. I want to stand on my head so badly, but I think I would most probably break my neck trying to balance on the staircase.

I feel in my pocket. I don't have my Oyster card. I can't even get home.

It's then that I see her, on the wall, looking down at me: a portrait of Nell Gwyn. Underneath is a brass plate that says *Nell Gwyn was a known customer of the White Swan*. Warmth trickles through me as I smile up at her.

'What shall I do now, Nell Gwyn?' I ask. I shut my eyes and the smell of oranges fills my nostrils.

I'm sitting on a stool, in the corner of a theatre dressing room. Half-dressed ladies in bloomers and bodices are painting their lips and cheeks red, laughing, joking.

One of them smiles at me in the mirror. It is Nell Gwyn. She turns.

'Go home, my little one,' she says. 'You should not be on your own in the streets of London town.'

'Can I stay with you?' I say. 'Please, can I live with you? My mum's gone, she's left me. You wouldn't leave me, would you, Nell?'

'I've got to go on stage, my lovely,' she says. 'The

king's watching tonight. I've got to act and dance for the king. I've got to make him laugh. Go home, Nell, go home,' she says, fading into the mist of time.

I open my eyes. A petal from the white rose I'm clutching flutters and blows in the spring breeze, down the stairs, and lands by the window. Nell Gwyn's telling me I must ask for help in the White Swan pub, the pub she used to drink in.

A man's wiping spilt beer, which is dripping from the top of the bar.

'Oi! We can't have kids in here!'

'Please,' I say, 'my mum was drinking in here, and now she's gone with my Oyster card, and I've got no money to get home.'

A girl with pink hair and a tattoo of an owl on her hand is collecting empty glasses. 'Is there anyone we can phone?' she asks.

'My Aunty Lou,' I say. 'I know her number.'

She takes her phone out of her pocket and hands it to me.

'Mum's gone,' I say to Aunty Lou when she answers. 'I'm in a pub in Covent Garden.'

'Are you with anyone?' she asks. I hand the phone to the pink-haired girl, who starts chatting to Aunty Lou.

When she rings off, she calls to the man behind the bar, 'Bob, is it OK if I walk her to Leicester Square Tube? Her aunty's going to meet her at Kentish Town.'

'Yeah, be quick,' shouts the man.

It's on the tip of my tongue to say to the pink-haired girl that I'm not a little kid, and that I'm sure I am quite capable of walking to Leicester Square by myself, but then *I see Nell Gwyn, as plain as day before me.*

She puts her finger to her lips and says, 'Ssh, Nell, you go with her, my lovely. I don't want you out on the streets of London town on your own, the hour 'tis getting late.'

'I'm Allie,' says the girl. 'You've got me out of collecting dirty glasses.'

Allie buys me a ticket when we get to the station. 'Will you be all right?' she asks. 'Just follow the signs to the Northern line.'

I nod, I am fine with the Tube.

I shut my eyes on the train as it rattles through the stations to Kentish Town.

Aunty Lou's waiting at the top of the escalator. Angry words about my mum are wanting to jump from her mouth, I can see, but she just hugs me.

We catch the bus up the hill. I snuggle into Aunty Lou's shoulder.

'Did you have a nice day?' she asks.

'It was a golden perfect day,' I say, 'till the end.'

'Well, just remember the golden perfect bit,' she says, giving me a kiss on the cheek.

Michael and TJ are finishing *Operation Ark* when we arrive home. It's a good thing Mum left the window open.

I feed my animal family and go to bed, but I can't sleep.

As a blackbird sings its song in the early morning dew, I finally hear Mum come in next door.

'Good night, Mum,' I whisper. 'Good night, Nell Gwyn, and thank you,' I whisper to the dancing shadows as I finally drift off in my dreams.

19

The sun wakes me, shining straight through the flowery curtains and into my eyes. Aunty Lou's bed's empty.

There's a note on my pillow. I squint at it.

I'm helping with the flowers at church
Hope you had a lovely sleep, my child.
Food in the fridge.
Love you xxx

I smile, then feel sick as I remember that Mum left me on my own in the White Swan pub.

I hear a thud and, 'MICHAEL! I AM GOING TO ACTUALLY KILL YOU!'

I squirm out from under the bed covers and run and open the bedroom door. My face smacks into a pair of jeans dangling from the ceiling. I push them out of the way and look up to see long lines of string across the ceiling, with socks, shirts, boxer shorts, T-shirts, hoodies, a pair of Aunty Lou's knickers, one of her best dresses and my parka, all dangling from them.

TJ is on the floor in a heap in the kitchen doorway, tangled in a spider's web of string, a pair of boxer shorts draped over his head.

Laughing, I try to untangle him.

'TJ, you'll be sorry for shouting at me when my invention takes off and I'm a multimillionaire.' Michael sits on the top of the washing machine. 'This genius string pulley will pick dirty washing off the floor and carry it all the way to the washing machine.'

TJ groans and puts his head in his free hand.

'Just think,' continues Michael, 'all that wasted time and energy spent carrying dirty clothes to the washing machine, which could be spent playing computer games, and grown-ups all over the world won't need to get vexed about their kids' messy bedrooms, so the world will be more peaceful. I most probably will get the Nobel Peace Prize, then you'll be sorry for shouting at me like that.'

'MICHAEL!' shouts TJ, trying to free his ankle from the string wound round it. 'My wardrobe's empty because of you. These clothes were clean and pressed, ready for me to go out looking my finest, and now I've no clothes to wear, nothing.'

There's the sound of the key in the lock. Aunty Lou stands in the open doorway, mouth open, gaping up at the ceiling.

'MICHAEL! What are my best dress and my undergarments doing hanging from the ceiling?'

'I am trying to help you, Aunty, so you don't get tired carrying clothes to the washing machine.'

'Michael, I am going to go into the kitchen to put the kettle on, and by the time it has boiled, I want all those clothes back where they belong. DO YOU HEAR ME?'

'Yes, Aunty,' says Michael.

'And, TJ, GET UP OFF THE FLOOR AND HELP HIM.'

'Yes, Mum,' says TJ, freeing himself from the last loop of string.

Aunty Lou fishes into her handbag for her Post-it notes and pen.

She writes:

YOU HAVE 10 MINUTES

Then Aunty Lou takes a deep breath, turns to me and smiles. 'Nell, have you had any breakfast?'

I shake my head.

'Come,' she says, and takes me into the kitchen, pours me a glass of mango juice and starts making pancakes.

They're scrummy. I eat tons of them, greedy as my guinea pigs.

Michael and TJ stomp around with piles of clothes in tangled string.

Aunty Lou runs me a bath with bubbles, while I set the food train in motion to feed my animal family, and it works perfectly. I then give them all a cuddle, sharing the love out.

Michael has taken the bathroom door lock off for one of his inventions, so now there's just a sign hanging from the door. I flip it round to read *KEEP OUT*.

While I'm in the bath, soaking my troubles away, I hear a knock on the front door. Then the bathroom door opens, and Mum comes in, and sits on the end of the bath.

I shut my eyes so I can't see her.

'Can't you read? It says *keep out*,' I say.

'Come home, Nell,'

'You left me,' I say. 'You went off and left me on our special day.'

'I'm sorry, Nell. I can't help it. I tried so hard, I really did. I wanted our day to be perfect, and it nearly was, but I just wasn't strong enough. Please, Nell, you know how it is sometimes, I get carried away and can't stop. I'll try harder, I promise. I won't do it again.'

'Mum, most kids want adventures. I just want normal,' and I hold my breath, and put my head under the water so it bubbles in my ears and I can't hear her *I won't do it again* lies any more. I wish I was Bob Marley – tortoises can hold their breath for a very long time, and they can smell through their throats. When I come up for air Mum's gone. Aunty Lou comes into the bathroom with her special sky-blue, fluffy bath towel. She holds it out for me as I step out of the bath, and wraps it around me. I bury my head in her shoulder and sob.

20

The tap-tapping of a crow's beak on the window jumps me awake.

One beady eye is looking through the gap in Aunty Lou's curtains, straight at me. A group of crows is called a murder. This makes me shiver. Time to get ready for school, then I remember it's half term and snuggle back under the covers but I'm hungry.

My tummy rumbles. I hear hushed voices and the rattling of cups coming from the kitchen. It's Gracie and Aunty Lou. I hear my name, and I've got to know what's going on, so I creep up to the door to listen.

'I just don't know what to do, Gracie, it's killing me. I don't know how much longer I can carry on. I feel it's my duty to report Stacey for neglecting the child.'

My heart stops. No she can't. Supposing I get

sent away from my animal family! I listen again.

'At least when she's here we can keep an eye on her. I think it's such a blessing that she can stay with you when things get bad,' whispers Gracie.

'Yes, but Stacey knows that. I worry that I am enabling her to keep drinking because she knows that I'm always there to pick up the pieces.'

'Do the school suspect?' asks Gracie.

I don't wait to hear the answer. My breath catches in my throat, and I feel like I'm drowning. I need air. I open the front door and run out into the courtyard, gulping the spring breeze as it wafts around me.

I run to the wall in front of the shops, and stand on my head. I see an upside-down van drive up, and an upside-down man opens the creaking back door of the van to get out a huge bundle of upside-down newspapers and walk towards Patel's. An upside-down Mrs Patel stands in front of me.

'Nell, please, come the right way up immediately. You'll hurt your head and get those lovely curls of yours so dirty.'

I crash land. Mrs Patel takes my hand.

'Nell, you must come with me.' And she leads me into the shop, and thrusts a copy of *North West London Tonight* into my hand, and there I am on the front page, smiling into the camera, with Felicity Cordour standing next to me, with her arm round my shoulder.

SCHOOL GIRL RESCUES FOX

Mayor Felicity Cordour awarded the Borough Nature Award to school girl Nell Hobs from the Beckham Estate, for rescuing an injured and distressed fox. Felicity said it was a pleasure to meet Nell, who is a credit to young people everywhere.

Mrs Patel is smiling down at me. 'Our lovely Nell, famous, on the front of the newspaper. Well, I think that deserves a free copy of *Creepy Crawly Fact or Fiction*.' She shudders as she looks at the picture of the slug on the front of the green-covered magazine as she hands it to me. I think most of my *Creepy Crawly Fact or Fiction* are free, 'cause Mum always forgets to pay her paper bill.

I take the magazine from her. 'Thank you so

much, Mrs Patel, that is most kind of you,' I say in my best, most politest voice. 'Slugs are fascinating creatures to us naturalists. Did you know that they have about twenty-seven thousand teeth, which, Mrs Patel, is more teeth than even a shark has, and it can stretch to twenty times its own length, to get through the tiniest of gaps.'

'Please, Nell, no more, no more! Slugs are the most revolting of creatures.'

'Mrs Patel, everybody has to have somebody to love them, even slugs.'

Mrs Patel suddenly looks so sad. 'They do, Nell, you are absolutely correct,' and she kisses me on the forehead.

I hear Mr Patel chatting to the newspaper van driver in the stockroom.

'Please can I have the newspaper to show Aunty Lou?'

'Take a few, they're free. Your mum will want one as well, Nell.'

I don't bother to reply to that comment as I snatch a few copies of *North West London Tonight* and pile them on top of my *Creepy Crawly Fact or Fiction* and leave the shop.

The van door is open a crack. I peep through and

there's a big bundle of *North West London Tonight* by the door, with my face on the front, smiling up at me.

I have to find my dad. Aunty Lou said she can't go on much longer. A plan grows in my brain. Time for action.

I look round the courtyard. There are two ladies chatting by the lift, but they're not looking in my direction. Some Beckham Street Boyz cycle past, whooping to each other. I wait till they're in the distance and I slip my arm all slug-like through the tiny gap between the van doors. I can't risk the door creaking. I grab the top of the string holding the pile of papers and try and turn it on its side, but it's too heavy to do with one hand. I'll have to risk the creaking door. I take a deep breath, pull the door open, grab the pile of *North West London Tonight* and run. Out of the corner of my eye I'm sure I see the curtain of number one twitch.

I don't stop running till I reach the wasteland. I can't risk the van driver seeing me and following me to Aunty Lou's. I've brought enough trouble to her door. I crouch down and wait and watch the van driver leave the shop, shut the doors of the van and drive off.

I've done it! It's not stealing, it's a free newspaper, I tell myself as I hide the bundle of papers in the middle of a bush and, grabbing the copies Mrs Patel gave me and my copy of *Creepy Crawly Fact or Fiction*, I head back to Aunty Lou's to feed my animal family and have some breakfast.

Michael answers the door wearing a long, black, curly King Charles II wig.

'Nell, where've you been?'

'I'll tell you later. What've you got that on for?'

'It came in the post to Gracie's. Don't I look fine?'

'Odds fish, you do,' I say, stepping into the hallway and shutting the door with my foot behind me. 'Michael, listen, you've got to help me. Does Aunty Lou know I went out?'

Michael shakes his head.

'Does Aunty Lou what?'

I look over Michael's shoulder to see her standing in the kitchen doorway.

'Aunty Lou, look,' I say, pushing past Michael.

I hand her the newspaper. 'I saw the van drive up to Patel's, and ran and grabbed a few copies.'

Aunty Lou beams at me. 'Oh, Nell, you look lovely. Front page and everything.'

'I've fed your animal family,' says Michael. 'The

wheel came off on Beyoncé's and Destiny's carriage and I needed to make some adjustments.'

'Well, I think this calls for a celebration pancake breakfast,' says Aunty Lou.

Michael and I follow her into the kitchen.

'Look at this, Gracie,' she says, handing her a newspaper.

'Oh, you take a lovely photograph, Nell. You'll have to show your mum.'

I don't reply, and just make myself terribly busy washing my hands, and then sit down next to Michael at the table.

'Michael, take that wig off.'

'Oh, can't I wear it for breakfast?'

'No,' says Aunty Lou, 'take it off, you'll get maple syrup on it.'

'I bet King Charles II was allowed to wear his wig for breakfast,' mutters Michael, as he puts it back in its box.

The pancakes are scrummy but Aunty Lou's words, *I don't know how much longer I can carry on*, burn in my heart.

'I think, Aunty Lou, that me and Michael should go for a walk on the wasteland. We need some exercise.'

'Nothing like a good walk for lifting your mood and putting a spring back in your step,' says Gracie.

'Good idea,' says Aunty Lou. 'Oh, and Nell, I've spoken to your mum, and she says it's fine if you stay here for half term, it'll give you both a bit of space, and give her a chance to get herself together, and do a few shifts at Bernie's, pay some bills.'

Relief floods me. A whole week without having to check if she's breathing, a whole week without having to look for hidden bottles. A whole week without Mum anxieties.

I pull Michael, clutching his wig box, into his bedroom. 'Michael, I have to find my dad. I just have to. I heard Aunty Lou telling Gracie that she'll have to report my mum and, Michael, supposing the authorities send me away from my animal family and and . . .'

'Nell, tell me what you want me to do?'

So I tell him my plan as we sit on the end of his bed, me cuddling Asbo and him cuddling Chaos, who's burying into the King Charles wig, which Michael's wearing again. 'So you'll have to change into your school uniform,' I finish.

'Nell, are you mad? It's half term.'

'Trust me.'

'Can I wear my wig?'

'No, you've got to look inconspicuous. Now, have you got scissors and glue?'

Michael crawls under his bed and brings out a pair of scissors, a black marker pen and Blu-Tack with fluff attached.

'That'll do,' I say, 'now meet me by the old youth club in ten minutes.'

After putting the scissors, pen and Blu-Tack into my school rucksack, I race out of the front door, all the way to the wasteland, and don't stop till I reach the bush I hid the bundle of newspapers in.

They're still there, thank goodness. The twigs scratch my skin as I pull them out. I ease the top three newspapers out of the bundle and, taking the scissors, I sit on the grass, and carefully cut out the article about me from the front page.

Michael, dressed in his school uniform, comes puffing up to me. 'Odds fish, I'm ready.'

'Odds fish,' I say, jumping up to join him.

'Michael, somewhere out there's my dad and I've got to find him. If we spread these pictures around enough, my dad might see and step forward, excited to have a daughter that's won the Borough Nature Prize and is famous, on the front page of the newspaper. And let's make sure my three dad options see it too.'

'To work,' says Michael, and we head towards the lift on the Beckham Estate. I press the button; as usual it takes, like, for ever to come. An old man steps out of the lift, pushing past us, muttering about *kids today*. Michael stands leaning against the door so it can't close as I stick my newspaper article and photo with Blu-Tack on to the metal side of the lift, next to the emergency button, 'cause finding my dad *is* an emergency.

'Now loads of people will see that. Good work,' says Michael. I draw an arrow to my picture with the black marker and write Is this your Daughter?

A man's voice. 'Quick, the lift's here.' I spin round and see Obo and two other workmen hurrying towards it. I pull a paper out from the bundle Michael's hugging.

'Obo, look, I'm on the front page of the paper. I won the Borough Nature Prize.'

'Well, isn't that something, Nell?' And he smiles at me.

'Please have a paper,' and I thrust it in his hands as the lift doors close.

'Do you think he looked proud?' I ask Michael.

'Well, maybe,' he says, shrugging his shoulders.

'I think I need to give him one more reminder.' I say, seeing Obo's van parked in the courtyard. 'Keep watch, Michael,' and I quickly put one of my cut-out articles behind his windscreen wipers.

'Oi! What are you kids doing?' It's the ginger-haired workman.

'Run!' yells Michael and we leg it towards Bernie's Burger Bar.

I peep through the door; the shop's empty but my heart jolts as I see Mum sitting at a table in the room at the back. She looks so tired and the demon's made her look much older than her years. Her cheeks look red and her skin so dry. She has her head in her hands as she's looking down at Bernie's big leather order book. Bernie's behind her shouting down the phone, 'No, don't put me on hold,' then he puts the phone on speaker and paces up and down, as annoying music like you get in supermarkets blares out of the headset.

'Distract them,' I say.

Michael nods, and goes into the shop, leaving the bundle of newspapers with me. Then he stands in the doorway of the back room so they can't see me.

'Hello, I was just wondering how you both are on this fine day?'

Bernie says, 'I'll be fine when they answer the phone.'

'I'm good, thank you, Michael. Where's Nell?' Mum asks.

'She's rescuing insects,' says Michael.

I slip into the shop and behind the counter. I take out one of my newspaper articles from my rucksack, and quickly Blu-Tack it next to the framed photograph of Bernie, his wife and all the little Bernies. This way he'll see that I could be a part of his family.

'Michael, why have you got your school uniform on, it's half term?' I hear Mum ask.

'I think it suits me,' says Michael. Mum snorts with laughter as I run out of the shop.

Then as I wait for Michael, who's now boasting about how he's going to be Charles II in the costume pageant, and everyone'll have to do as he says, I feel so sad, 'cause I want to tell Mum that I'm on the front page. But I'm too angry with her, and pride stops my words.

I grab one of the papers, run back into the shop and leave a copy of *North West London Tonight* on Bernie's counter. At least she'll see that I'm on the front page of the newspaper.

I duck down behind the wall outside the shops and wait till I hear Michael's footsteps. I jump up to join him and we take turns to lug the bundle of string-tied papers towards the bus stop.

On a tree is a big colourful poster, advertising the Celebrate Heritage Day.

The poster shows lots of men on horses, in feathered hats, with a man in a helmet banging a drum in the corner. I shiver inside as I look at it and Michael squeezes my arm.

'Odds fish,' he says, grinning, 'that'll be us at the head of the parade.'

We pass more and more posters in shop windows and on lamp posts. Some people even have them in the window of their houses.

Some girls on the bus, who I recognise from year nine, giggle when they see Michael in his school uniform. We ignore them and hop off when we reach school. I leave a copy of *North West London Tonight* on my seat, 'cause you never know who might see it.

We squeeze through the forbidden shortcut, and leave the bundle of newspapers behind the old girls' changing rooms.

'Oh, I'm not sure about this. I don't like it, Nell.'

'Michael, you've got to. Please. Look, Mr Richardson's window's open. I'm going to duck down and watch. Mr Richardson and Miss Gordon catch up on paperwork the first part of half term. Miss Gordon's always moaning about how lucky we are to get a holiday.'

We link thumbs and say, 'Odds fish.'

Michael shrugs his shoulders and walks off towards the school office. I crouch low and run towards the head teacher's window, stepping over the flower bed. I kneel down outside his window and peep through. Mr Richardson frowns as he types into his computer. He's singing a Beyoncé song to himself! I have to bite my lip so I don't giggle. There a knock at the door and I see Miss Gordon walk through with her hand on Michael's shoulder.

'Michael Henry to see you, Mr Richardson. He forgot it was half term,' and she leaves the room snorting with laughter.

Michael stands in front of Mr Richardson's desk.

'Oh, Michael, Michael, what are we going to do with you? Your head in the clouds as usual?'

'Actually, Mr Richardson, sir, my head is in numbers and when I won that Leonardo award, it said I have a mind that needs encouraging, so I was wondering if you could help me with a maths problem?'

'Very well.'

'Please could we do it in my classroom, 'cause your office makes me nervous, sir. I can't think straight, 'cause I'm usually in trouble when I'm in this room.'

Mr Richardson laughs and shuts down his computer. 'Very well, lead the way, Michael. As a matter of fact, I miss teaching since I became head teacher.'

As soon as they leave, I push the window further up, and clamber through. On Mr Richardson's desk is a copy of *North West London Tonight*. He's already seen it. He must be very proud that I'm on the front page.

I scrabble in my rucksack for the last cut-out article and Blu-Tack, and I stick it on the wall, next to the photograph of the three little Richardsons with their violins. Maybe he'll see that I should be in that photograph, as his daughter playing a trumpet. I bet I would be good at playing a trumpet. As I step backwards, I knock something on to the floor.

I turn round to see what it is. No word of a lie, I swear I stop breathing. It's the latest copy of *Creepy*

Crawly Fact or Fiction, the one with the slug on the front.

Mr Richardson really could be my dad. I hear Miss Gordon leaving her office, her footsteps come closer.

I quickly climb back out of the window, and head for the school playground.

Mr Richardson's voice floats out of the half-open window of our form room. I duck down and crawl on my hands and knees till I'm underneath the window sill. I pull myself up so that just my eyes are peeping over the top. Mr Richardson is pacing back and forth.

'So, Michael, as you can see there's beauty and logic in numbers.'

I duck down and rummage in my rucksack for a pen. Tearing a page out of my maths book, I write in big letters:

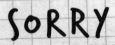

When Mr Richardson has his back to me, I hold it against the window. Michael's gazing through the window, chewing the end of his pen. He sees me and mouths, 'GET ME OUT OF HERE.'

I duck down and think fast thoughts. I cannot

rush into the classroom, and say there's an emergency and that Michael's to come home, or Mr Richardson'll investigate, and we don't want Mr Richardson to think there's an emergency at number five or number six Beckham Estate. No, Michael'll just have to stay there and do the maths lesson. I write on the back of the paper:

IT WILL NOT BE FOR EVER.
HE'll WANT HIS DINNER.
JUST TRY AND LOOK INTERESTED SO HE
DON'T SUSPECT. I'M GOING TO TARKEY
HOUSE ESTATE

Michael mouths, 'Nell, don't!'

Mr Richardson turns towards the window and I duck down.

No word of a lie, I feel guilty for leaving Michael, but I've got a job to do. Gracie's words, 'Do the school suspect?' ring in my ears. Mr Richardson must never suspect anything. It's not like Michael'll be stuck in there for ever, is it, I tell myself.

Grabbing the bundle of papers from behind the old girls' changing room, I head towards the bus stop, the string digging into my hand. I take a deep breath: now for the Tarkey House Estate.

When the bus stops outside the estate I leave a copy of *North West London Tonight* on my seat again. I get off the bus and take a deep breath as I enter the courtyard of the Tarkey House Estate. I haven't been here since I was best friends with Chantal, who lives on the fourth floor. I see Kyle kicking a ball against the sign on the wall that says **NO BALL GAMES**. He has his back to me. I make my way towards a bench, and sit next to an old man who's fallen asleep. I cut out my article from one of the papers. I shut my eyes to calm my anxieties, 'cause I can't stand on my head in the middle of Tarkey House Estate, now, can I?

I listen to the sound of dogs barking, kids crying and there's a man shouting somewhere. I hear the chirps of a pair of robins marking their territory.

Nell Gwyn swims into my head. '*Nell, you should not be in this part of town that is not yours to step in.*

'*I've got to find my dad, Nell Gwyn, he might well live here, it stands to reason.*'

I head for the lift and I try to wedge the door open as I stick my picture on to the wall of the lift and write Is this your Daughter, but I'm not quick enough. The doors close and the lift starts going up. It stops on the fourth floor, and when the doors open Chantal's mum, Trina, is standing there.

'Nell!' she says. 'How lovely to see you. Are you here to see Chantal? She's in the flat with Tanya,' and she gives me a hug, pulling me out of the lift as she steps in. 'We saw your picture in the paper, very nice.'

The doors close and she's gone.

Chantal lives at number twenty-eight, which is the flat next to the lift. Her bedroom's at the front, her window's open, and her voice is coming out loud and clear.

'Nell will really think she's something, now she's in the paper.'

I put my back flat against the wall and inch closer to listen.

'When Mr Samuels sees your costume, though, Chantal, he's gotta let you be Nell Gwyn.'

'Thank you, Tanya.'

I inch closer still, peep through the gap in Chantal's window blind and have to bite my lip hard so I don't laugh.

Chantal is wearing the biggest, frilliest, most massive pink dress that I've ever seen. Lace bloomers peep out from the bottom of her dress and she has the biggest, floppiest pink bonnet round her head. She looks like Little Bo Peep, not like Nell Gwyn in the slightest. I feel warm inside as I think of my own fine costume.

'*As if I would ever adorn myself with such foolish garments,*' *scoffs Nell Gwyn, pushing me away from the window.* '*Now, make haste and get away from these abodes.*'

I head towards the lift and press the button. As I step in, I tread on my face. The picture's come off the lift wall. I quickly get some more Blu-Tack out and stick it back. I'm just pushing down the last bit of Blu-Tack when the lift reaches the ground floor.

When I step out the lift, Kyle and Craig are wheeling round in front of me on bikes, wearing yellow bandanas.

'OI, HOBS, WHAT YOU DOING HERE? THIS IS T CREW TERRITORY,' shouts Craig, and they start wheeling round me faster and faster.

'*Hold your head up high,*' *whispers Nell Gwyn.* '*Don't let them see the fear in your eyes.*'

'I can go where I want,' I say, 'move out of my way. I've got things to do.' I step forward, but Kyle's bike misses my toes by a millimetre.

Faster and faster they circle round me, their bikes skidding, front wheels rearing up in front of me, spraying grit in my face, stinging my cheeks.

'Oh my days,' shouts Craig, ripping the string-tied bundle from my hand, 'she's walking around carrying old newspapers, just 'cause her ugly face is on the front for rescuing that old fox.'

'GIVE THEM BACK!' I scream as he rides away.

'No,' says Kyle and, snatching them from Craig, he pulls the newspapers from the string, and throws them everywhere, so they are flying through the air. One lands in a puddle. I run to try and grab it, before it sinks. I feel a shove in my back and I fall, mud splattering my face, as my knees and hands sink into the cold mud. My rucksack slams against my back.

'Pick the lady's papers up now.' I feel a strong pair of arms lift me on to my feet. I look down at the hand that grabs me – *Rich* is tattooed on the knuckles.

I look up into the face of Richie Lane, leader of the T Crew. Next to him is Michael, fear in his eyes.

'Any friend of Prof M is a friend of mine; this boy's a legend down these ends. That was pure jokes, him making that clock whizz round with a remote control in his maths class, I'm telling you, we laughed for weeks. That Mrs Hubert hated me when I was at school, hated me, she did.'

Craig and Kyle are scurrying round picking up my newspapers, their bikes lying on their sides on the ground, with the wheels still whirring round.

They hand the newspapers back to me. Richie grabs one and whacks them round the head with it.

'Don't you ever show Prof M or his little friend disrespect again, do you get me?'

'Yeah, Richie. Won't happen again, Richie.'

'Nell, I came as quick as I could. Are you all right?'

I nod. And we run out of the Tarkey House Estate and don't stop till we reach the bus stop.

'I want to walk home,' I say, 'then I can give these last few papers out. You get the bus if you want, Michael. I've dragged you around enough today.'

'Oh no, I'm not leaving you. It felt like I was stuck with Mr Richardson for hours, Nell. I only got away 'cause he had to take a phone call, otherwise I reckon I'd still be there. You shouldn't've gone to the Tarkey House Estate without me.'

We trudge home in silence, me handing out newspapers to passersby.

'That's my picture on the front,' I say over and

over. 'I rescued a fox. I won the Borough Nature Prize,' but no one says, 'Nell, my long lost daughter!' I sit on a wall and cut out my article from the remaining few papers, and writing Is this your Daughter, stick them on trees, underneath posters for a missing, cross-looking, one-eared tabby cat called Jackson.

I hope they find Jackson.

I hope I find my dad.

21

My anxieties build as Thursday, Friday, Saturday and Sunday of half term all tick by, and no one steps forward to say, 'Nell, I'm your dad.' That's four whole days. Hundreds of people must've seen my photograph, thousands even, but not one person comes to say they're my dad. I stay at Aunty Lou's, avoiding Mum.

I keep myself busy taking Bob Marley, Asbo and Chaos to the wasteland every morning with Michael, and we lie on the grass, laughing and talking about him becoming a famous inventor, and about his chats with Leonardo da Vinci.

Finn asks me to take Buster for a walk every afternoon. I saw Aunty Lou talking to him, so I think she put him up to it. But Finn says I'm a big help to him, and that Buster behaves a lot better with me than he does with him.

'That's 'cause I'm a naturalist,' I say.

I do feel better out on the wasteland with Nell Gwyn by my side, running over the grass, free as a bird, with Buster at my heels.

But on Monday morning when it's time to start school again, I wake up and my thoughts won't come, like my brain's filled with mashed potato, and my legs feel heavy, like there's a thousand years of troubles pressing down on my toes, and I can't even stand on my head.

'It's time for school,' says Aunty Lou, but it feels like she is far, far away, and that her words are lost in a cold foggy forest of letters.

Her words repeat in my head, but they hide behind trees making no sense.

I hear her call TJ. He comes and scoops me up with the quilt wrapped round me and carries me into Aunty Lou's special front room, with all the Jesuses and the pretty angels.

My Borough Nature Prize silver cup shines at me, next to Michael's trophy on the mantelpiece where I asked Aunty Lou to keep it safe.

I hear Michael clattering about as he feeds my animal family. Aunty Lou brings me in a cup of hot, sweet tea. 'I think, my Nelly, you need to stay at home and have a looking-after-yourself day.'

Michael leaps through the door. 'Can I stay off school and look after myself too?'

'Stop with your nonsense,' says Aunty Lou, as she pushes him out into the hall. I hear the front door bang and Michael shouting across the courtyard, 'Hello, Daniel, Mr Samuels, sir.'

'Won't be a minute,' says Aunty Lou as she hurries out of the room.

I close my eyes, wanting this still, quiet minute to last for ever.

Something warm and furry snuggles into me.

I open my eyes. It's Tutty, Mary's little spaniel. Sir and Aunty Lou are standing over me. Aunty Lou holds a pink plastic tub filled with crayons. Daniel – sir – is carrying lots of big sheets of paper.

'Nell,' says sir, 'I think you should work from home today and I've a special job for you. Well, two special jobs, actually. It's a good thing I stayed with Mum last night because you're the very best person I can think of for these two jobs. Job one, please will you look after Tutty as my mum has to go to the chiropodist? Job number two, we need someone to draw some posters to advertise Celebrate Heritage Day.'

I feel my lips move into the tiniest twitch of a smile. I know sir's just being kind to me, as there are already proper posters for Heritage Day, but I nod and hold out my arms for the little dog, who licks me on the nose, then jumps off the sofa, running round the room, sniffing at things and wagging his tail.

I catch Daniel and Aunty Lou smiling a secret smile at each other.

'Thank you, Daniel,' says Aunty Lou. 'That'll keep you busy, won't it, Nell?' Then she sees sir out.

I hear them talking on the front door step.

Sir asks, 'Is there anything I should know?'

I hear Aunty Lou choose her words carefully.

'I think that sometimes we all have to get off the carousel of life for a moment and look after our minds, but, know this, I have Nell in my care and that makes my heart easy, having her where I can keep my eye on her. I need to do that with every breath in my body.'

'I can see how much you care for that child. If there's any more I can do . . .'

Words like 'school can be overwhelming' and 'a rest'll do her good' drift through the air as they chat on the doorstep.

Tutty snuggles up to me as I lie on my belly on

the green carpet, and I draw King Charles with long, raven-black hair, exactly the same colour as mine.

Aunty Lou brings in a plate of toast and another cup of tea. She lays a large plastic sheet underneath me and the crayons. 'So there's no messing up my carpet. No crumbs,' she says. 'I'll just be in the kitchen.'

'Thanks, Aunty Lou,' I say.

I hear her singing along to the real Bob Marley (not the tortoise!) and I join in, singing about not worrying about a thing, and about how everything is gonna be all right.

But the words don't work on me. I don't think Bob Marley had a mum like mine.

The fog in my brain thickens, so I stand on my head, but the plastic feels all slippy underneath my hands. As I try to balance, Tutty thinks it's a game and jumps up at me, barking, so I flop down and start to work. I try to imagine all my worries up in the clouds as I take special care drawing each curl in King Charles's hair.

I'm sitting on a throne, in a beautiful dress, with a crown on, and my dad, King Charles, is drawing a picture of me, his daughter, his princess.

Chantal Smith's dad calls her his princess. I've

never been anyone's princess, not ever.

I draw the finest hat with a red feather that swishes and swirls.

Next I draw Nell in a pretty yellow dress, with a basket of fine oranges. Tutty keeps walking on the paper and trying to grab the crayons in his teeth. As I colour in, my thoughts begin to slowly unfreeze.

Not Obo, not Bernie, nor Mr Richardson's come forward to claim me. No one who might've seen my picture on the tree, or in the lifts, or on the bus. No one. I finish my toast, and drink my cooled, sweet tea. Aunty Lou's still singing as she bangs around in her kitchen and Tutty has fallen asleep, curled up on my picture of King Charles. I wander through to Michael's room to get Bob Marley. I let the tortoise crawl over my pictures, slowly, slowly.

I draw another picture of Nell, holding her son upside down out of the window, and the king with a speech bubble coming out of his mouth, saying, 'Save the Earl of Burford!'

An idea prickles.

'Get dressed quickly,' calls Aunty Lou.

I scramble into my clothes.

Tutty's awake, so I pick him up and give him a cuddle as I look out of the window. Bernie, from

Bernie's Burger Bar, smiles and waves as he walks across the courtyard. Obo is striding along with a bag of tools. He stops to adjust his green woolly hat, smiles and winks at me as he walks to his van. I try to wink back but I'm not very good at it.

My dad's somewhere out there in the world, but where?

'These pictures are good, Nell,' says Aunty Lou, looking at them all laid out on the plastic sheet. The sun's shining through the window, lighting them up so the colours glisten.

She brings our coats in with a dog lead from the hall and clips the lead on Tutty's collar. 'We're going out,' she says.

I hear a car draw up outside.

I open the front door. Mum's sitting in the back, waiting.

'Waterlow Park please,' says Aunty Lou to the bald cab driver as she gets in the front. 'Come on, Nell, don't just stand there!'

The sounds of clanging metal and men shouting to each other are coming through the air. I can see in the distance that scaffolding's being built round the old youth club.

'Nell, come on,' says Aunty Lou, so I have no

choice but to climb in the back of the cab, with Tutty on my knee.

'I think it's always good to sort things out on neutral territory,' says Aunty Lou. 'I know the park and the house are significant to you both. Stacey, I remember you taking Nell when she was little to the art workshops, so it's somewhere you have both had good times and, besides, it's a beautiful day to go to the park.'

Mum smiles at me. I don't smile back. We sit in silence all the way and stand awkwardly, not looking at each other, as Aunty Lou pays the cab driver.

'Come on!' says Aunty Lou and marches into the park, Mum and I trying to keep up behind her.

I let Tutty off the lead and he tries to run after two squirrels chasing around on the grass.

We sit on a bench. The wood feels warm beneath my jeans, but my heart feels cold.

'Stacey,' says Aunty Lou, 'Nell is a blessing in your life, and time and time again you let her down. Nell, what would you like to say to your mum?'

My bones ache with hurt as I look at them both, saying nothing for what seems like years. Then my words come firing out, like bullets from my tongue.

'When I got my nature prize, it was my special

moment,' I say. 'I wanted you to be so proud of me. And then you came to parents' evening drunk. How could you? And then, after our golden day, you leave me alone like that, in the pub. You're meant to be the one looking after me, Mum.'

Mum has tears pouring down her cheeks.

'I'm so sorry, Nell. I try, honest I do. It just takes over me. I'm begging you to give me another chance. My life's nothing without you.'

Mum holds out her arms to hug me, but I can't quite hug the hug of forgiveness back. Not yet.

'Nell, give us five minutes,' says Aunty Lou.

I call Tutty, who comes bounding up with his tail wagging. I clip his lead on and hand the end to Aunty Lou. A sudden cool spring breeze blows through my hair, so I snuggle into my parka as I walk away from them, towards Lauderdale House.

Nell Gwyn dances through the trees ahead of me, leaves in her curls. She blows me a kiss and vanishes.

I run up the stairs to the long, yellow room, where Nell Gwyn held her son out of the window by the ankles and King Charles claimed him, saying, 'Save the Earl of Burford!'

The tiny prickle of the idea I had when I was drawing my picture grows into a twinkling star, swelling into a fireball that becomes the sun. A brilliant sunshine of an idea. Mum and I are no good on our own. Nobody came forwards from me having my picture in the paper. I need dramatic action to give my dad the courage to step forwards.

The costume parade will finish at the old youth club, where they're putting up scaffolding.

Everything starts to slot into place. Supposing Michael were to hold me upside down from the scaffolding at the youth club during the costume pageant and ask for my dad to come forwards. I decide then and there to keep my idea secret for the moment, though. I'll have to find the right time to tell Michael.

I look through Nell Gwyn's window, down on to the bench, where Mum and Aunty Lou sit.

Aunty Lou has Mum cradled in her arms, like a baby. My heart aches as I watch. Aunty Lou sees me and waves.

And suddenly I want to be with my mum so badly, I run down the stairs, and out into the park, to the bench.

'I love you, Mum,' I say and hug her.

And once again I let her into my heart.

Nell Gwyn peeps from behind a tree and smiles at me, and my heart sings.

22

That evening Mum helps with *Operation Ark*, but this time moving Beyoncé, Destiny, Fiz and Tyrone, Aunty Lou hamster, Bob Marley and me back to my own bedroom.

'Thanks so much for looking after my Nell,' she says, as she puts Bob Marley in his tortoise table. 'But from now on it's my job and I intend to do a good one.' And she hugs Aunty Lou and TJ.

'Come here,' she says to Michael, 'I'm so glad my Nelly has you as a best friend.'

He stands there looking awkward, his arms hanging by his sides, as she pulls him into a hug. 'Your mum would be so proud if she could see you,' Mum whispers into his hair, and he flings his arms round her and hugs her back.

'Use the walkie-talkie if you need to chat,' whispers Michael when I see them out.

'Odds fish,' I say.

They all disappear next door, and it's just Mum and me and my animal family.

'Honest, Nell,' says Mum, 'this time I mean it.'

'*Pinkie promise*,' I say.

'*Pinkie promise*,' she says, and we link our little fingers with love.

'Look,' she says, and she's so proud as she opens the kitchen cupboards to show me packets of cereal and tins of sweetcorn and baked beans, all stacked up, and in the fridge is fresh milk and cheese and those small cartons of apple and orange juice.

'I've been working hard at Bernie's so's I could do a big shop for your return. And look at this,' she says, and shows me a pile of clothes, all ironed and pressed, ready to go back in the wardrobes and drawers.

'I've put money on the key for the electric meter,' she says.

'So you won't leave me alone in the dark?'

'No,' she says, looking so sad. 'I won't do that.'

'Well done, Mum,' I say, kissing her on the cheek.

Mum and I do a treasure hunt, like we did when I was little at Easter time, before the demon came to stay, only we're not hunting for chocolate eggs, we're searching the flat for all her hidden, nearly empty bottles of drink. I find one in the cooker, the airing cupboard and even one between the cushions of the sofa. I make myself busy, splashing the contents down the plughole. When she's not looking I search again, just to make sure there are no more hidden in unexpected places. I see her looking longingly at the door sometimes but she doesn't go out of it.

And Mum tries, she really does. For two whole weeks she goes to work and comes back home. There's always food in the cupboards, clean washing in my drawers and kind words from her lips, and I love her with my whole heart.

I don't see Nell Gwyn. In my thoughts and dreams it's just Mum and me. Me and Mum. Stacey and Nell. Nell and Stacey.

Friday of the third week of Mum not drinking is a brilliant day at school. Mr Samuels told me that the posters I'd drawn were so good they were going to use them for publicity for the Celebrate Heritage Day costume pageant, around the school. They were printed into proper posters, on glossy paper, by the IT department and I had to sign them like a proper artist, and Mr Richardson gave me five merits, which is the most merit marks I've ever got in my whole life. I wonder if he gives his own children merit marks at home for doing the dishes and the hoovering.

Happy memories dance in my brain as I run home from school ahead of Michael, with the poster of Nell Gwyn in my hand to show Mum. I'm being careful not to squash it, and I run, run across the courtyard fast . . . then everything slows down. I see the police and ambulance carrying a stretcher with someone on it, and it is my flat that they are coming out of, and people are watching and some are crying and . . .

'MUUUUUUUM!' I scream, and my poster flies out of my hand and flutters to the floor, and a policeman steps backwards on to it, and Aunty Lou reaches out her arms to me and she's crying, and there are arms everywhere, reaching, reaching for me.

'MUUUUUM!' I scream again.

'Nell, child, your mum's very ill,' says Aunty Lou. 'Do you want to go in the ambulance with her?'

I nod.

Someone helps me up into the ambulance and Mum is just lying there, still. When I lean forward and kiss her cheek, I smell the drink on her.

'Mum, you *pinkie promised*,' I say and I try to link

my little finger with hers, but I can't 'cause her hand is lifeless, so I kiss her pinkie tattoo.

I hear a dog barking. It's Buster. My animal family! They need me. Supposing they take them away while Mum is in hospital.

'I can't go. Please let me out,' I say.

'Nell, Nell, look at me.' It's Gracie. 'It's all right, I'll go to the hospital with your mum,' she says, stepping into the ambulance. 'You stay here with your Aunty Lou.'

My legs wobble, TJ grabs me, and lifts me down from the ambulance, but as they close the doors and drive away panic fills me.

'I SHOULD'VE GONE WITH HER!' I scream. I try to run after the ambulance, but my legs collapse on to the floor. A stranger lifts me on to my feet.

I need to get home, my animal family'll be hungry,' I say. 'Bob Marley needs his lettuce.' I push the stranger's arms away and run towards my flat, but our front door's been broken down, and a policeman blocks my way.

'Excuse me,' I say but he ignores me.

'Nell, darling child, come with me,' Aunty Lou says oh so gently. 'Jesus and the angels will look over your mum.'

'But she should be home with me,' I say and I know that I need to have a word with those angels up in the sky. I shake Aunty Lou's arm off and run to the lift. I hear her calling after me but I jump in and I go up, up, up to the eighteenth floor, towards Jesus and the angels. I run out of the lift, along the balcony and I kick over the sign that says **ENTRY PROHIBITED**. I run up the stairs to the roof and I walk to the edge.

I see tiny people below. I can see the wasteland and the old youth club, but I want to be up in the clouds so I can have a word with those angels. I reach my arms out, wishing I could fly but I can't, so I reach them up, up towards the sky where Aunty Lou says the angels live.

'HELLO!' I shout up to the sky. 'Can you hear me? My name is Nell, please look after my mum, she is very ill in the hospital. Her name is Stacey. Please, please, please look after her.'

'Come away from the edge, Nell.'

I turn. It's Finn and TJ. They walks towards me, slowly.

'Please, Nell,' says TJ, and his voice cracks. I run across the roof and jump into his arms and he holds my legs tight, as I reach, reach up, up, up, towards where the stars will shine at night time.

'PLEASE LOOK AFTER MY MUM,' I shout.

'MUUUUUUUUUUM,' I cry. 'MUUUUM. I LOVE YOU.' I try to jump out of TJ's arms high, high into the sky to reach the angels.

'I've got you,' he says. 'I will always catch you, Nell.'

And as TJ carries me down from the roof, the scent of oranges fills the air.

23

TJ holds me tight in his arms all the way down in the lift, till we're standing in the courtyard looking at my flat.

Michael's waiting for us, his face all crumpled. He reaches out for my hand and TJ holds the other as we watch *Operation Ark* being done for what could be the very last time, by a lady from the RSPCA.

'She's just here to help you,' says TJ. 'The police had to call the RSPCA when they realised there were animals in your flat, when they broke the door down.'

And as Bob Marley, Asbo and Chaos, Beyoncé and Destiny, Fiz and Tyrone and Aunty Lou hamster are carried out of my flat and into Aunty Lou's my whole world crashes.

Aunty Lou's front door is open and I see her having a heated conversation with a man with sticking up hair, wearing a blue check shirt and jeans. As my world spins I hear words: 'cannot be separated', 'animal family', 'needs to be with those she knows', 'I will look after her while her mum's in hospital'.

The man in the blue check shirt walks up to me.

'Hi, Nell, my name's Rory, I'm from children's social care. Are you happy to stay with your Aunty Lou while your mum's in hospital?'

I nod. 'Just till Mum is better,' I say. He starts to talk to me, but my brain feels foggy, and I just watch his mouth go up and down, and it's just words, words, words. 'Sorry,' I say, 'I have to go to my animal family.'

Rory walks with me to Michael's bedroom.

The lady from the RSPCA sits next to me on the edge of Michael's bed.

TJ is clearing all Michael's inventions into boxes and carrying them next door to his bedroom. The room looks strange and empty.

'Hi, Nell, my name's Molly. Your animals are so beautifully looked after, I can see they're in very good condition.'

'I'm a naturalist, I make sure that my guinea pigs and my tortoise get lots of fresh grass to exercise on.' I say, 'I take them to the wasteland,' 'They're my family.' I say. 'They've taken my mum to the hospital.'

'I know, pet,' says Molly, and she helps me feed my animal family.

Aunty Lou pops her head round the door. 'I'll be responsible for Nell and all of her animals while her mum's in hospital.'

Molly gives her leaflets, and says any time she needs support to call. Aunty Lou thanks her, taking her hand, as if she doesn't want to let go.

Through the fog that fills my brain, there is talking, talking everywhere, and phone calls and people, people I don't know. Rory, the man in the blue check shirt and sticking up hair, is talking to Aunty Lou again.

Michael comes into the room.

'Nell, I want you to have my bedroom, as long as you need it, so you can sleep with your animal family.'

No words come, so I nod my thanks.

'Aunty Lou's going to take you to the hospital. Are you ready?'

I nod again.

Michael sits next to me on the bed. 'I want you to have this,' and he presses a small brooch with a picture of an angel into my hand. 'Mum gave it to me before they took her to the hospital in Jamaica. She called me Michael after the angel in the Old Testament. She said the angel on the brooch would look over me, now that she couldn't look after me any more. It's painted by Leonardo da Vinci. I want you to take this to the hospital, so the angel can look over your mum.'

I look down at the brooch and into my friend's kind brown eyes.

'Thank you, Michael,' I whisper.

Gracie is waiting for us at the hospital.

'It's this way,' she says. And she takes us past the rows of sick people in beds, into a room where Mum's lying with a bandage round her head. There are tubes coming out of her and bleeping machines, and she's so pale and still.

A nurse who's checking one of the machines turns round and smiles.

'Talk to her,' she says.

I sit in the chair next to the bed.

'Michael gave me this angel to look after you,' I say, and I show her Leonardo's angel, even though she can't see it, and I put it on the cabinet, next to her bed, so that it can guard her.

'Keep talking,' says Aunty Lou, but I don't know what else to say.

So I say the first thing that comes into my head.

'*Ride a cock-horse to Banbury Cross, to see a fine lady upon a white horse. Rings on her fingers and bells on her toes, she shall have music wherever she goes.*'

'Mum used to say it to me so that I would go to sleep,' I say, 'but I'm saying it to her so she wakes up.'

A woman in a blue dress comes into the room. 'Hello,' she says. 'I'm Doctor Cuthbert, would you like to come this way?' and she takes us into the family room.

'I understand a workman found her,' says Doctor Cuthbert.

'Yes,' says Aunty Lou, 'Obo. He came round to put some shelves up for Stacey, and saw her collapsed on the floor through the kitchen window. He called the emergency services, and knocked on our door to let us know.'

It was Obo. He kept his promise. I'm glad he found her. Obo's kind, but if he were my dad surely he would be at the hospital with me now. But I can't think about that now.

'Your mum has alcohol poisoning,' says Doctor Cuthbert. 'She had a seizure and blacked out and hit her head. She's very sick, Nell, but we're all doing our very best for her.'

She starts to explain how alcohol affects every part of the body, but I feel as if all my anxieties are sitting on my chest and I can't breathe.

I go and sit next to Mum again.

'Mum,' I say, 'I got five merit marks for the posters I drew and they printed them up on shiny paper and everything, and I signed them like a proper artist.'

I do not know if she can hear me, but I'm glad I remembered to tell her about my five merit marks. They seem like a hundred years ago now.

When it's time to go, I wrap my little finger round hers, even though she can't link it back, and I whisper into her ear, 'Good night, Mum. I love you.'

24

I feel all jittery when we reach the Beckham Estate. My flat lies cold and empty, next door to Aunty Lou's. The demon has won.

Aunty Lou opens her front door and I walk into Michael's bedroom. The bed's been newly made with clean, pale-blue sheets and a cloud-patterned quilt. I crawl under the covers, still in my school uniform, and curl up in my sky bed while Aunty Lou holds me tight.

The phone rings.

A pause as TJ answers. He calls Aunty Lou to the phone and my legs go all tingly and I can't be still. This cannot be happening. No, no, NOOOOOOOOOOOO and Asbo is doing guinea pig singing and I'm up, Asbo in my arms and, before Aunty Lou sees me, I run out of the door and I can't stop.

I run, run, run, my feet pounding the pavement.

I have to run faster, run back to happy times. Waterlow Park, sitting on the bench, hugging Mum, telling her I love her, and Nell Gwyn dancing through the trees, winking at me, blowing sweet kisses.

I hold my guinea pig close and run, winding through the roads, and I'm on Dartmouth Park Hill, running up to the park, my legs on fire. A lady with a little boy wearing a blue coat, on a scooter, turns to stare.

'Are you OK?' she calls, but I don't stop. I don't answer. I have to get to the park and, as I run through the gates, I sink down behind an oak tree. All's quiet as I look up at the house, at the window, where Nell Gwyn held her son by the ankles in front of the king. The sound of breaking twigs: it's the little boy in the blue coat on the scooter, staring down at me.

'I like your guinea pig,' he says, pointing at Asbo.

'You can hold her,' I say, putting Asbo in his arms. 'I need to stand on my head.' And I do, with my legs up against the tree, till my thoughts go away and I can't stand on my head any more.

'Hector, Hector. Where are you?' calls a woman's voice.

'Is that you?' I ask, taking Asbo back.

The boy nods.

'Don't tell anyone I'm here. It's a secret,' I say, putting my finger to my lips.

The boy giggles, puts his finger to his lips too, gets on his scooter and then his blue coat vanishes through the trees.

I hug my knees to my chest and watch the window as it starts to go dark.

As the moon comes out and the shadows dance, I see her, Nell Gwyn, watching, watching me from the window, then she vanishes.

And as I close my eyes a warm blanket of love surrounds me.

'There are folk looking for you, my pretty little Nell,' she whispers in my ear. *'Stay safe with me till they come for you,'* and in the moonlight, she sits on the grass with me under the tree. *Nell Gwyn and me. Me and Nell Gwyn, Nell and Nell,* and a tawny owl sits on a branch and watches us and my napping guinea pig, as torch beams shine through the trees accompanied by calls of, 'Nell, Nell, Nell, where are you?

Then Buster leaps on top of me, barking, licking me.

'Found her!' Finn calls through the trees and he sits on the ground where Nell Gwyn has now vanished from, and he takes off his coat and wraps it around me as I shiver.

'There are a lot of people looking for you, Nell. They care what happens to you in here.' He thumps his heart. 'And Buster, he knows you need him.'

Sasha comes through the trees and sits under the oak tree on the other side of me.

She kisses me on the cheek and she gently takes Asbo from my arms.

'Let Buster keep you warm,' she says and I put both arms around Buster, who licks my tears away.

And the police come and take me back to the Beckham Estate.

'I can smell oranges,' says Finn, and I smile a secret almost smile.

Back in the warmth of her flat, Aunty Lou feeds me hot soup like I'm a baby. Buster stands guard.

'They used to call Staffies the nanny dog,' says Aunty Lou, 'and, child, I can see why. The way that dog loves and protects you.'

There's a silent scream in my belly, spiralling into the deadly whisper of guilt. Round and round it spirals, faster and faster, until out it comes, in massive sobbed words.

'It's my fault,' I say, 'if I'd been there to check her breathing. If only I'd stayed home from school. If I'd not been so mean to her when she drank . . .'

'If, if, if, if, if. Did you lift the drink to her lips?'

'No, Aunty Lou, but . . .'

'There is nothing you could have done, child,' says Aunty Lou. 'You did not cause this, you cannot control her drinking. Only your mum can do that. She has the illness of addiction, and she loves you so much, but she's so ill, my darling. So very ill.'

'Will she wake up?' I whisper.

Aunty Lou pauses. 'We don't know yet, darling. The doctors will do everything they can for her.'

And I nod and fall asleep in the sky bed, to the sound of Asbo and Chaos guinea pig chatting, and Aunty Lou hamster's wheel going round, and Buster never leaves my side.

25

Aunty Lou takes me up to the hospital on Saturday. There's a man selling flowers by the side of the road.

'Stop,' I say, 'please, I want to buy some flowers for Mum.'

Aunty Lou hands me ten pounds and I slip out of the cab, and buy a big bunch of white roses. Just like the ones I scattered for Nell Gwyn with Mum on our golden day in London.

My heart start to feel heavy as each step brings me nearer to Mum's hospital bed and the bleeps of the machine get louder. Aunty Lou takes my wobbly hand and holds it tight.

A red-haired nurse is checking the bleeping machines and tubes.

'Hello, Mum,' I say, 'I've brought you some flowers.'

'I'll sort those for you,' says the nurse, smelling

my white roses, 'they're beautiful.' She smiles at me. 'Keep talking to her,' she says.

'I'm going to read *Creepy Crawly Fact or Fiction* to her,' I say, 'so that she can hear my voice.'

The nurse looks at the picture of the snail on the front of my magazine, and shudders. 'Interesting choice of reading material,' she says, 'but you just keep talking to her.'

Aunty Lou goes to find a doctor, while I read to Mum about snails.

'Did you know, Mum,' I read, 'when it's dry, a garden snail will hibernate in its very own shell and it actually seals the entrance, hibernating for several months, sleeping away . . . but, Mum, don't you sleep for several months, please wake up, Mum, please, please open your eyes.'

Aunty Lou comes back into the room, followed by a team of nurses including the red-haired nurse.

'They're going to wash and change your mum, make her comfortable, so we'll go for a walk, come on.'

'We won't be long,' says the red-haired nurse with a smile.

Aunty Lou leads me to a bench by the pond in the hospital grounds. On a leaf is resting a male emperor dragonfly. I know it's a he as it has a sky-blue abdomen. I break off a dead twig that's casting a shadow over the dragonfly 'cause they need to warm up in the morning sun, before they go flying for the day. It flies up, hovers in the air and then lands on my head.

'That's good luck. Make a wish,' says Aunty Lou.

I close my eyes. *Please, please, please, get better, Mum and never, ever have a drink again*, I whisper in my head. I hope that counts as one wish not two.

If a dragonfly had landed on my head a week ago, I would've wished for my dad to claim me, but now all my wishes have to be for my mum.

When we get back to Mum's hospital room we bump into Sasha. 'I hear music is proper good for people who are in hospital,' she tells us, 'so if it's OK with you I've come to sing some songs to your mum.'

I grab hold of her arm and lead her to Mum's bed.

'Hello, Stacey,' says Sasha. 'I've come to sing to you.'

'Mum likes Beyoncé,' I tell Sasha.

Sasha slips into the chair next to the bed and holds Mum's hand and starts to sing that song about haloes, and as her voice dips and soars and fills the room with such beauty, Aunty Lou joins in and harmonises, and then I join in too and I see *Nell Gwyn, peeping through the window, with a smile on her face.*

The nurse comes back in and stops to listen to the singing, along with some of the other nurses, and Doctor Cuthbert puts her hand on my head and smiles, saying, 'If music be the food of love, play on,' which I think must be something Shakespeare said.

A rainbow of sparkly-dressed people start coming into the ward, next to Mum's room. I realise it's the Zebra Blue Community Choir. Sasha waves to them.

'All these people wanted to come to make music for your mum,' says Sasha, smiling. 'There's not room in here for the choir but she'll hear it.'

If Mum could see this, she would be so happy, 'cause she hates dull clothes.

A lady with a cardboard box full of tambourines and other percussion instruments smiles at me.

'Join in, Nell,' she says.

I pick a wooden stick with lots of little silver bells on, because of our special ride a cock-horse rhyme. *Rings on her fingers and bells on her toes. She shall have music wherever she goes.*

Sasha walks to the front of the choir, and they start to sing that song about how we all need somebody to lean on. I join in, shaking my silver bells that sound like Mum's laughter.

The patients in the beds are sitting up and clapping. The choir's taking requests.

'BOB MARLEY,' shouts out Aunty Lou, and soon everyone's singing about not worrying about a thing, but it's when we're singing that Beyoncé song about single ladies, and waggling our hands in the air, that Aunty Lou calls out to me.

'Child!' And I turn and see Mum's eye flicker, just for a second, but I saw it.

'Mum,' I say, 'Mum,' and I sit on her bed, and wrap my little finger till it squeezes round hers and, for a zillionth of a second, she squeezes back.

26

'Your mum's a survivor,' says Doctor Cuthbert to me in the family room, 'but she's done a lot of damage to herself, especially to her liver, and the road towards recovery is long. You do understand that, Nell, don't you?'

I nod. 'But there's hope that she'll wake up completely. She squeezed my finger, honest.'

'Yes, Nell, that's a positive sign but do keep talking to her.'

'Go and see your mum,' says Aunty Lou, 'I'm just going to have a quick word with the doctor.'

But I don't go straight away, I stand outside the door, with my ear squashed against it.

There are a lot of mumbled words, but then I hear Dr Cuthbert as clear as day say, 'If Stacey drinks again, her chances of survival are small.'

And the bottom falls from my world.

I hurry along to Mum's room, and I talk to her and don't stop. Mum has to wake up. I tell her about Nell Gwyn visiting me in my dreams. Me running through the morning rain, with Buster at my side. I tell her about Michael, on the wasteland, playing, talking, laughing with Asbo, Chaos, Bob Marley and me. And I read to her from *Creepy Crawly Fact or Fiction* till my voice is nothing but a whisper.

I go to school and I manage to do my lessons, honest I do . . . until we get to geography. We learn about Australia, and how it is far away, on the other side of the world. I think about Mum in the hospital bed and how far away her brain must be, and I want to be with her, to bring her back from wherever she's hibernating, not sit in school learning about Australia. And then I can't help it . . . I stand on my head in the middle of the classroom, so I'm upside down like Australia. My class are laughing and shouting, and Mr Boswell's red in the face, but I don't care 'cause I need to stand on my head.

Miss Gordon takes me from the classroom, and calls Aunty Lou to come and get me from school, and that evening Miss Petunia phones Aunty Lou and they talk long into the night.

Rory from children's social care calls round to

Aunty Lou's, and tries to get me to talk about how I'm feeling, but I can't, so I stand on my head in the middle of the room, and he just looks at me, and then goes and talks to Aunty Lou.

Every evening I read to Mum. On one Thursday evening, at two minutes past six o'clock, I look up and her eyes are open. Aunty Lou calls for a nurse, and they come running. When Mum sees me for the first time she cries.

She tries to speak. I put my ear close to her mouth.

'I'm so sorry, my little Nell,' she whispers.

'Don't cry, Mum, I love you,' I say.

Over the next week, Mum gradually comes out of hibernation, and gets stronger.

It makes me so happy to see her smiling and out of bed and sitting in a chair, wearing her own clothes. She still has an oxygen tube running up her nose and she is weak and thin but she looks like my mum again.

Doctor Cuthbert comes in and introduces us to a man with mousy hair and a goatee beard, wearing a T-shirt that says *STEP FORWARD FROM ADDICTION* on it. He's carrying an iPad.

'This is Rankin, who you spoke to on the

telephone, from the Alcohol Advisory Bureau,' says Doctor Cuthbert.

'Hi, everyone,' says Rankin. 'Shall we talk in private?'

'No,' says Mum, 'I want my daughter and Lou to hear what I have to say.'

Mum looks me in the eye. 'I am an alcoholic,' she says.

And that word *alcoholic* coming from Mum's lips for the first time punches my breath away. It is both terrible and beautiful to hear, 'cause admitting it to herself has to be the first step to getting better, right?

'Stacey, you were very brave when we spoke on the phone earlier. Have you thought more about what we spoke about?'

'I have,' says Mum, 'I phoned you because I want to make that commitment. I want to stop drinking, but I can't do it alone. I want to go on a rehab programme. There, I've said it.'

Hope flutters in my heart. Aunty Lou and I perch ourselves on the bed.

'That's where I come in,' says Rankin. 'It can be hard to get a place in rehab but I'm going to do my best. OK?'

Mum nods.

As Rankin looks down at his iPad, I can't help but peep over his shoulder.

There's a list:

Rose Wood Rehab

Malwood Rehabilitation Centre

Star and Gate House Addiction

Then at the bottom of the screen I see it: **Orange House Rehabilitation Programme**.

I feel a shiver in my belly. 'This one, please.'

Rankin touches the link.

I read from the screen. It says they offer 'detox support, therapies and integration back into the community and life skills programmes'.

Aunty Lou takes a look. 'Nell, it's in Yorkshire.'

Mum holds her hand out for the iPad and, as she reads the screen, she smiles the smile of hope.

Nell Gwyn peeps at me from behind Mum's hospital curtain.

'That place is groundbreaking,' says Rankin. 'It's on the Yorkshire Moors, they go for long walks, do horse-riding, gardening, that sort of thing. Its philosophy is *Strong body, strong mind*.'

'You are the mother of a naturalist. It's perfect,' I say.

'I'll make a call,' says Rankin and he disappears.

Mum chats to Aunty Lou and Doctor Cuthbert, while I walk up and down *with Nell Gwyn by my side*, trying to resist the urge to stand on my head, 'cause I don't think they allow that in hospitals. 'Please, please, please let there be a place for Mum,' I say over and over.

Rankin comes back with a smile on his face.

'What luck, a bed's just become available,' he says.

Nell Gwyn winks at me as I rush to hug Mum.

27

I wake up thirsty, in the middle of the night. Us naturalists have to keep hydrated. I slip on my tarantula slippers and purple dressing gown and pad to the kitchen, but the light is on. I can hear Aunty Lou's voice on the telephone.

'Gracie, I don't know how we're going to get the money these things cost, and then there's all her unpaid bills . . .'

My heart thuds to my feet. Aunty Lou's talking about Mum.

'She'll qualify for some funding but still . . .'

Of course we need money, the Orange House Rehabilitation Programme won't be free. Mum and I are such a bother to Aunty Lou. I bet at times she wishes that we didn't live next door. She's so kind and all we do is cause her problems. I shake my *Ark Fund* jar; a few coins jangle. Not enough for rehab, but it's something.

I take my jar to the kitchen. Aunty Lou is no longer on the phone, but sitting at the kitchen table with her head in her hands.

'Nell,' she says, 'you should be in bed.'

'Aunty Lou,' I say, shaking the coins from my jar on to the table. 'A start for Mum's fund.'

'Oh, Nell. I don't want you to worry. We'll think of something. You keep your coins for your pet food. TJ's bought you some bits and pieces to be going on with.'

She opens a cupboard door and it's full of gerbil food, hamster food and guinea pig pellets. Such kindness takes my words away.

I creep back to Michael's bedroom. Aunty Lou hamster is whizzing round on her wheel. I take her out of her cage to give her a snuggle in the dark. How are we going to get the money?

For the first time since Mum's been in hospital I think about how different it would be if I had a dad. I would go and live with him and not be such a problem to everyone.

Putting Aunty Lou hamster back in her cage, I pull the window blind up to look at the stars. There are zillions of them, like my zillions of problems.

I stand on my head, looking at the upside-down stars, before curling up in my sky bed and trying so hard to get to sleep.

Over the next week, there are lots of hushed phone calls, whispered words, soppy sympathy looks from people round the estate, from strangers, saying how sorry they are. Why are they sorry? It's my mum. And my anxieties rocket about Mum's rehab, and even standing on my head doesn't work for long. By Sunday morning I feel like I'll burst, so I run down to the Music Project and start banging hard on the drums.

And I hit the drums harder and harder, faster and faster.

Sasha stands and watches me till I can't hit the drums any more.

'Feeling better?' she asks.

'A bit,' I say.

'Come and look,' says Sasha.

I follow her out into the courtyard.

'We're having an Orange Day fundraiser. Every shop and market stall and supermarket have donated oranges to the Stacey Hobs Rehab Fund.'

In the middle of the courtyard is a white van, and

Finn and TJ are unloading the boxes of oranges and Willem, Gracie's grandson, is filling baskets with them. From the stairway and across the wasteland they come, lines of children, some with their own baskets, some bags, and as Willem fills them they start to call, 'Oranges, who will buy my oranges?' and, 'Oranges for sale!'

Front doors open and there's a song in the air made up of all the different languages spoken on our estate, as people buy the oranges. Bernie sets up a fresh orange juice stall and Aunty Lou, Gracie and Mrs Patel serve people drinks.

'It was your Nell Gwyn costume that gave me the idea,' says Sasha. 'By the way, I owe you one. I got an A* for my project.'

I feel choked, I can't speak, so I squeeze her hand. Everyone doing all this to help pay for rehab, so Mum can get better.

Michael comes running over, wearing an orange shirt and black bow tie.

'I bet you I sell more oranges than anyone,' he says. 'Can't stop, I've got to get going.'

I have guilty thoughts. Michael's such a good friend to me, and I've hardly talked to him recently, what with Mum and everything.

Bernie brings two glasses of orange juice over to Sasha and me.

'There you go, my diamond girls. Nelly, don't you go hungry or thirsty, you hear, you know where I am. You come to Bernie.'

King Charles's words flash through my head. *Let not poor Nelly starve.*

I give Bernie a daughter-like smile, willing him to say, ''Cause your dad don't want you to go hungry,' but he doesn't, he just walks back and carries on serving orange juice. I imagine what it would be like to be Bernie's daughter – a life-time supply of chips would be good, and he's a kind man giving my mum a job and everything. But if he were my dad, he'd have come with me to the hospital. I banish that thought. Maybe he's just too busy, I tell myself.

A car drives up next to us and parks. It's Chantal and her mum, Trina.

'How many times, Chantal? You're not having a spray tan. Now, get out of the car and show some kindness,' says Trina.

Chantal looks over at me and half-waves then looks away, but she walks over to Willem and fills her basket full of oranges.

Trina leans out the window.

'Anything you need, Nell, you just let me know. I mean it, anything.'

'Thanks, Trina,' I say. She always used to give me nice teas and caring words, when I was friends with Chantal.

In the distance I see Mr Richardson and Mrs Hubert walk on to our estate. Michael quickly walks in the other direction with his basket of oranges. Napoleon brushes himself up against Mr Richardson's legs and the head teacher picks him up and cuddles him. Napoleon don't usually let strangers pick him up, let alone cuddle him. Mr Richardson's definitely a good naturalist.

Mrs Hubert bossily starts organising the queue of children waiting to fill their baskets from the van, like it's the dinner queue at school.

Mr Richardson walks up to me and smiles. Mr Richardson never smiles at the other kids. He hands me a purring Napoleon.

'Nell,' he starts and in my head he's saying, 'My daughter, I have passed my love of animals to you. We shall go on safari to Africa to meet the lions.'

But he doesn't, he just says, 'We're all here for you, Nell.'

'Mum's sitting up now in the hospital,' I say. 'You

could go and see her if you want.'

Mr Richardson looks really uncomfortable, and he starts asking Sasha how she's getting on at performing arts college. I bet if I were Mr Richardson's daughter he would make me do extra homework, even in the holidays.

I spot Obo in the distance, and run up to him.

'Hello, my girlie,' he says when he sees me.

'Thanks for calling the ambulance,' I say, 'and thanks for keeping your promise to Mum.'

'Nell, that was the least I could do,' says Obo, but in my head he's saying, 'My daughter, I shall build you a tree house as high as the birds, and you can watch them in their nests. It will be the best tree house ever, with room for all your animal family. Room for your mum when she comes out of hospital and room for me to move in, so that we can live together as a family.' I just know he could help Mum and me rebuild our lives. But he doesn't say any of those things, he just carries on walking up to the van and helps Willem stack the empty crates.

TJ announces over a mic, 'It's time for the Beckham Estate's Got Talent show.'

Everyone cheers. A crowd's gathering as people stream out of the lift and stairwell.

Finn plays his guitar, Sasha sings and I stand on my head and everyone claps.

People are walking around with buckets labelled *The Stacey Hobs Rehabilitation Fund* and the coins are jangling in.

I take a bow, and next two girls start Irish dancing.

Aunty Lou brings old Mary out in her wheelchair to watch. Tutty's in her lap. I run over to them.

Mary's clapping her hands to the music. 'I used to be a professional dancer, you know, danced them all, *Swan Lake*, *The Nutcracker*, *Sleeping Beauty*. Though you wouldn't think it to look at me now, would you?' she says, stretching out her leg to look at her old crooked foot. 'I trained for the ballet at Tring Park which is the house where it's said Nell Gwyn used to visit the king.'

I lean over and give the old lady, who has danced in the very same rooms as Nell Gwyn, a kiss on the cheek.

'You've got pretty feet yourself,' says Mary, 'very dainty.'

'Like Nell Gwyn's,' I say, laughing.

I look up to see people crowding into the courtyard from outside our estate. The music's attracting loads of attention. The courtyard's packed, it looks like the whole of north west London's here, and I see so many people dropping money into the buckets. Mary grabs my wrist and pulls me close. Her deep blue eyes spark deep into mine.

'Your mum will find her way, and you must follow your heart to find yours. But be warned, sometimes what we seek lies with us all along.'

What does that even mean? I think, as she releases her grip. I swear, it's like she can see into my thoughts. I smile at the old lady, 'cause I don't want to be rude and I concentrate on stroking Tutty's ears.

As the talent show finishes, as always happens on our estate, it descends into a party.

'Mum will be able to go to rehab, won't she, Aunty Lou?'

'It looks like it, child, yes. People are good.'

I give her a hug, every bone heavy with relief.

'Your mum doesn't want you to visit her today, she wants you to have a day off, and that's strict instructions,' says Aunty Lou.

'All right, it's a deal,' I say.

Even though I'm choked up at people's kindness, I suddenly need to be alone with my thoughts.

Everybody's been so amazing, helping Mum and

me out. But their kindness can't go on for ever, and then what will become of me? I can't be separated from Tyrone, Fiz, Aunty Lou hamster, Asbo, Chaos, Beyoncé, Destiny and Bob Marley.

I wander down to the wasteland. A piece of paper blows along the ground, catching on my foot. I bend to pick it up. It's a flyer for Celebrate Heritage Day. The man on horseback stares up at me.

My tummy cartwheels as I remember my plan to get my dad to claim me. I fold the poster up and put it in my pocket.

As the wind blows my curls, the full force of the realisation that Mum's going to the Orange House Rehabilitation Programme in Yorkshire hits me, but I just feel empty, as my life stretches in front of me without her.

28

On Monday I return to school.

Michael walks on my right side and *Nell Gwyn on my left*, like bodyguards.

'*You throw yourself into your learning to forget your woes*,' *she whispers in my ear.*

When I walk into my classroom, everyone falls silent and looks at me. Even Chantal Smith and Tanya don't have a word to say.

All morning teachers keep asking me if I want to go to the Thinking Room, but I don't want to think. I want to forget.

The bell rings for break and, as the chaos erupts around me, Mrs Hubert shouts at Michael about something, but her words just sound like noises in my head mixing with children's chatter and the smash of a ball against the window, and I've got to get out of there, so I run straight out into the playground, banging into Miss Petunia.

'Whoa, Nell, careful.' She smiles at me. 'Actually, I'm glad I bumped into you. I need your help, come with me.'

She takes me out to the school's vegetable garden.

'I thought you would like to give our garden some love and attention.'

She sits on a bench and sips a coffee, watching me as I lie on my belly, pulling the weeds up from around the carrots. Burying my hands in the soil feels good. An earwig scuttles over my arm.

I whip out my jam jar and let the earwig crawl in there, and then I take him over to a hollow in a tree.

'There you are, little fellow; you sleep in there. They're nocturnal, miss, he shouldn't be awake.'

It is good to feel like a naturalist again.

'Miss, some people think they're called earwigs 'cause they can crawl into your ear and lay eggs in your brain, but even though they *could* do that, miss, they wouldn't like it in our ears 'cause there isn't food for them in there.'

'Is that a fact?' says Miss Petunia. 'Ah, here's Michael.'

'Nell, I've been looking for you everywhere,' he

says as he comes running up.

'I'm going to leave you to it,' says Miss Petunia, and I watch her hurry back over the playground.

I think now is the time to tell Michael my plan, where no one can overhear us. I take a deep breath.

'Michael,' I say. 'I need your help.'

And I tell him the idea that's been burning a hole inside me.

'You know when we went on that picnic, and we were told that story about Nell Gwyn holding her son by his ankles out of the window, and how she said to the king, "Unless you give my son a title, I shall drop him." So King Charles ran forward to catch him and said, "Save the Earl of Burford."'

'Yeah, I remember,' says Michael.

'Well, I need you to do that to me.'

'Do what?' says Michael.

'At the pageant, hold me upside down from the scaffolding surrounding the old youth club and announce that you'll drop me unless my dad claims me.'

'Are you mad, Nell? How do you know your dad'll even be there?'

'Please, Michael, I've told you, I think my dad might be Obo.'

'Yeah, I like him,' says Michael, 'he's given me some good advice about constructing my inventions.'

'Or my dad could be Bernie.'

'That could be cool. A life-time supply of chips.'

'Or it could be Mr Richardson.'

'Oh, not that again, Nell. I am not coming to your house for tea if he's your dad,' says Michael. 'Sometimes, Nell, you are just too much.'

'Shhh, Michael, someone might hear. I saw him rescuing a spider and he even had a copy of *Creepy Crawly Fact or Fiction*, on his desk and, wait for this, he went to a Beyoncé concert with my mum.'

'This is mad, Nell. It doesn't mean nothing.'

'Look, if it's not one of those three, word is that people are coming from miles around to see the pageant, so there's a good chance my dad will be in the crowd. Now Mum's going to rehab, but what happens afterwards, what happens if she starts drinking again? I can't stay at Aunty Lou's for ever.'

'Why not?' says Michael.

''Cause I do nothing but cause you all bother and, you never know, I still may get taken into foster care. I can't be parted from my animal family, I just can't, and supposing I'm not allowed to take Asbo, Chaos, Fiz, Tyrone, Beyoncé, Destiny, Aunty Lou hamster and Bob Marley with me.'

Michael stares at me, looking really worried.

'Oh, please, please, please, Michael. You're King Charles II for the day, and everyone listens to the king of England.'

Slowly, slowly a smile spreads over Michael's face.

'Yeah, they'll listen all right, 'cause I am King Charles. OK, we can practise,' says Michael. 'Have the walkie-talkie by your bed.'

'Odds fish, it's a plan,' I say and we link thumbs.

After school, Aunty Lou is waiting for me at the school gate.

'Your mum's being transferred today. We need to get you to the hospital to say your goodbyes.'

Mum's sitting in the chair waiting for me, her bag packed. She looks so pale and thin and fragile as a butterfly's wing, and her breath is rattly.

'Nell,' she says, 'I know that you'll be the best Nell Gwyn ever in the pageant, and you'll do us Hobs proud.'

'I wish you could see me, Mum.'

'So do I, my Nelly nell nell.'

'*Time to go*,' *Nell Gwyn whispers in my ear*.

I hug Mum goodbye so gently, as it feels like she

might break, and I know with every breath in my body and beat of my heart, I have to let her go, so she can start her recovery.

Nell Gwyn brushes a tear from my cheek as I look back and wave one last time.

29

The night before the pageant, at two o'clock in the morning the walkie-talkie bursts into life. '*Odds fish*.'

'*Odds fish*,' I say back. I'm already dressed in my jeans and red owl jumper. My bed covers were pulled right up to my neck, just in case Aunty Lou checked in.

The flat is silent; the only noise is the hamster wheel spinning round.

I open the door. Michael's already waiting for me.

He puts his finger to his lips. I grab the petticoat of my Nell Gwyn costume and stuff it under my jumper.

As we sneak out of the front door, the hinge creaks. We hold our breaths but no one calls out to us, so we continue on our way.

I keep my fingers crossed that there's no one wandering around outside. That's the trouble when you all live on top of each other like we do, it would just take one nosy person to see us and it could get back to Aunty Lou.

The coast is clear. I shut the door behind us slowly. A pair of green eyes glint in the dark. It's Napoleon. He purrs and winds his way around my ankles as I try to walk, nearly sending me flying.

'Go home, Napoleon,' I whisper, but he totally ignores me and follows us all the way to the wasteland.

The old youth club looms ahead. We hurry across the grass till we reach it.

The sound of talking and laughter rattles though the dark. There are some Beckham Street Boyz cycling towards us. We run to the old youth club and duck down near the scaffolding. I hold my breath.

They race past.

I breathe out.

'We're in luck,' says Michael. 'I overheard Obo say that the Beckham Street Boyz vandalised the scaffolding alarm. It's not working.'

'Come on, we need to practise getting up there,' I say.

I pull my Nell Gwyn petticoat on over my jeans, so that I can practise climbing with my costume on.

It's really tricky. I keep treading on the hem. My foot slips and I bang my knee hard on the metal bar.

Michael shimmies up ahead of me with no trouble, then reaches down and hauls me up to a wooden platform level with an air vent in the old youth club wall.

'This is perfect,' I say. It's just high enough for the crowds to be able to see and hear us.

'You're too slow, Nell,' he says, 'we'll have to do it again.'

We climb back down the scaffolding to the bottom.

'Right, this time we'll climb faster and, when we get to the platform, I'll practise holding you upside down. The only way this'll work is if we climb up here so fast we surprise people.'

'It's hard with this petticoat.'

'Well, if you want this mad plan of yours to work, you're going to have to be quicker.'

'It's not mad, Michael. I want to find my dad.'

'It is mad and I don't like it. We're going to get into so much trouble.'

'Are you saying that you won't do it?'

Michael doesn't answer. Desperation ties my belly in a knot.

'If you care about me you'll do it.'

Michael looks as if I've punched him in the stomach and I wish I could swallow my words back.

'Care about you! Care about you? I do nothing but care about you. I have given you my bedroom and, look . . .' He delves into his briefcase and pulls out my Noah's ark charm bracelet. 'I bought it back from Percy's Pawn Brokers shop for you with money my dad gave me.' He throws it on the grass and his face is all twisted. I've never seen him like this before.

Noah, the silver giraffes and all the other animals glint at me under the stars as I swoop down to rescue my precious bracelet.

'Oh, Michael! Thank you from the bottom of my heart for this. I didn't mean to hurt you. I just want to find my dad, you wouldn't understand – you have yours . . .' I reach out to him, but he shakes my hand off.

'Oh, right,' he says, ''cause I hardly ever see him and when I do it's so awkward, and I don't know what to say to him. And then there's my mum having her mind put back together in Jamaica.' A single tear trickles down his cheek. 'I miss her so much.'

'I didn't know you felt like this.'

'Well, maybe that's 'cause you've never asked.'

He's right. I'm a horrible person. That day on the school bench when Michael was looking up at the clouds, so sad, all I did was bring the subject back to me finding *my* dad.

'Michael, I'm sorry.'

But he storms back across the wasteland, leaving me all alone in the dark, standing on my head in the moonlight.

30

No word of a lie, I don't think I've been asleep for more than ten minutes when my alarm clock goes off.

The memories of last night kick me in the stomach. Michael left the front door on the latch for me. But when I crept back in through the dark, the door of TJ's room was firmly shut.

I pack my Nell Gwyn costume for school but spot dirt on the hem of the petticoat from our practice last night.

I scrub at it but I make it worse, so I scrub harder, and with each scrub I think, *Will Michael forgive me?* Scrub, *Will he help me carry out my plan?* Scrub, and by the time I've finished with it, the petticoat's all damp.

'You're up early, Nell. Why are you so eager to get to school?' Aunty Lou pulls a chair out for me at the kitchen table. 'Eat.'

'I want to get to school before everyone else. I don't want my Nell Gwyn costume to get squashed.'

I take three bites and some gulps of juice, just to please her.

'I've got something for you,' says Aunty Lou, and she reaches into the cupboard and brings out a beautiful basket filled with sweet-looking oranges and covered in vine leaves.

It's the perfect finishing touch to my Nell Gwyn costume. I fling my arms around her. 'Thank you, Aunty Lou!'

She kisses the top of my head. 'This is your big day, and I know your mum'll be thinking of you, every minute of it.'

Before I leave, I tear a page out of my maths book. I scribble a note for Michael and shove it under TJ's bedroom door.

> Michael,
> Sorry, I didn't mean what I said.
> You're the best friend ever.
> Please, please, help me.
> Nell X
> P.S. Don't be late for school

When I get to school the atmosphere is electric with people chatting about what they're going to do in the summer holidays. I go straight to the biology lab to ask Miss Petunia if she'll keep my costume safe for me. As I struggle up the stairs, trying not to stumble on my costume, I hear Mr Samuels calling me.

'Nell, I'm arranging a meeting point for everyone in the pageant at breaktime. I'm just off to the office to see which room is free. So listen out in assembly.'

'Thanks, sir,' I say.

'Oh, and Nell, we've had some exciting news. The *City Bizz News Show* are sending a presenter and cameras down to film it.'

'I'm actually going to be on TV, sir?'

'You are, Nell, you are.'

My brain ticks. This means even more people will be watching, so there's even more chance of my dad seeing me.

Let's hope Michael's forgiven me and will help me with my plan. My feelings are so confused. I feel like running around squealing like Asbo and Chaos.

Miss Petunia is sorting through piles of papers when I walk into the biology lab.

'Ah, Nell, I'm just clearing stuff for the last day of term.'

'Please can I leave my Nell Gwyn costume here, miss? I don't want it to get crumpled.'

She smiles at me. 'Course you can. I'm so looking forward to seeing everyone dressed up.' She pauses. 'How's your mum doing?'

'She's gone to rehab. I had to say goodbye.'

'How are you feeling about that?'

And it's like a firework goes off in my heart, letting out all my secret, most hidden thoughts. I just explode with sobs.

'Miss, I am a horrible person.'

'Oh, Nell, of course you're not.'

'Yes, miss, I am truly horrible. Since I've been living at Aunty Lou's I miss Mum. I miss her so much and now she's gone far away to get better and I won't be able to visit her every night. But sometimes I feel so relieved that I don't have to check up on her all the time. And I don't have to worry any more about whether there is enough to eat . . . and I shouldn't even be telling you this. It's like I'm betraying her.'

Miss Petunia pulls up a chair and takes my hand in hers.

'Nell, it's really important you express your feelings, you're not betraying her. It wasn't your job to look after your mum. It was her job to look after you. But she loves you, Nell, I know – that's why she's gone to get herself better. She loves you with all her heart and you have to hang on to the good times you had together, so you can move your life forward.'

I swallow back my tears. I need to move my life forwards by finding my dad. And today is the day.

'Would you like to stay in here for a little bit, Nell?'

'Yes please, miss,' I say, relieved that I can hide out a little longer in my favourite room in the school.

I spend the next hour helping Miss Petunia sort through the lab for the end of term. My heart jumps when Michael runs breathless into the biology room, but he can't quite look at me.

'We've got our pageant meeting now in the assembly hall,' he says. 'QUICK!'

I grab my costume and my basket of oranges, and follow Michael to the assembly hall, but when we get there it's empty.

We stand and wait, the silence of awkwardness between us.

'Did you get my note?' I ask.

Michael nods.

'No word of a lie, I wanted to bite my tongue off for saying what I did.'

He look at me and grins. 'I shouldn't have left you out in the dark like that. I'm sorry.'

I take a deep breath. 'Will you do it?'

There's a forever pause then Michael links thumbs with me.

'Odds fish, I will.'

We wait and wait but still no one comes.

'Michael, are you sure it's in here? Who told you?'

'Chantal Smith,' he says. I turn cold.

'Michael, I bet she's told us the wrong room! Quick, we've got to find out where the meeting is. Run!'

31

We hurtle into the office. Miss Gordon tuts.

'Miss, please, where are we meeting for the pageant?'

'It's in your form room,' she says. 'HURRY, YOU'RE LATE.'

We run to our form room, and there stands Chantal Smith, wearing her ridiculous Nell Gwyn costume, with the biggest basket of oranges you've ever seen, and announcing at the top of her voice, 'Nell can't even be bothered to turn up, sir, but I won't let you down, Mr Samuels. I'll be the best Nell Gwyn ever, far better than Nell Hobs.' But as she's speaking, the class start to giggle.

I look to see what they're laughing at. Chantal's nose is turning bright orange, and her face has orange and white streaks across it, and is getting oranger by the minute. Her arms are smeared with bright orange patches. Chantal Smith's turning into a pink frilly giant orange!

'What are you all laughing at?'

The class laugh louder. Michael's actually rolling on the floor laughing.

Tanya takes a small make-up mirror out of her bag and holds it in front of Chantal's face.

Chantal screams. 'The tanning cream! I found it in the back of Mum's cupboard. Look what it's done!' And she starts to wail.

'Chantal, you can't mess around with that stuff. You got to put it on proper,' says Tanya and she starts to laugh too.

'I thought you were meant to be my friend, Tanya. Stop laughing!' screeches Chantal.

Mr Samuels claps his hands.

'Quiet class, please. Chantal, they did not have tanning cream in Nell Gwyn's time, nor did they have glittery talons on their fingers.' Mr Samuels points to Chantal's hands.

'These are glittery nail extensions, sir,' says Chantal with a scowl.

Mr Samuels shakes his head in total disbelief.

'You'd better go and see Miss Gordon, in the office, and show her. Nell Hobs is playing Nell

Gwyn, and that's the end of it.'

Chantal flounces out of the classroom, slamming the door behind her.

'That's shown her. The little baggage,' whispers Nell Gwyn in my ear.

I smile as I change with the others. My petticoat's almost dry.

As I walk towards the coach I hear someone call my name. It's Rulla running towards me. She pulls me to one side.

'I wanted to say goodbye. I leave school today.' She whispers in my ear, 'I know how you're feeling. My dad's in rehab,' she says and turns a cartwheel and is gone.

'Good luck,' I call after her.

Dressed in our costumes we all pile on to a coach that's waiting for us. Michael looks fine in his black wig and silver buckled shoes.

I curtsy to him. 'Your Majesty.'

He takes my hand and squeezes it as we sit at the front of the coach, just behind Miss Petunia and Mr Samuels, who is dressed as a Cavalier.

'Thank you, Daniel, I mean, sir,' I lean forward to say. 'This day is really important to me.'

He turns round and smiles his faded smile, and

then we all cheer as the coach drives off. I perch my basket of oranges on my knee to stop them rolling down the aisle of the coach.

When we arrive at the wasteland, the coach parks in a roped-off section of grass. I see the TV cameras and crew from the *City Bizz News Show* bustling around. My tummy does a cartwheel. Everyone in the country will see me playing Nell Gwyn in the pageant. Felicity Cordour, dressed in a purple skirt and jacket, her mayor chain glinting in the sun, is having her lipstick retouched. She sees me and gives a little wave. The cameras roll and an interviewer with a mic starts asking her questions.

There are Roundheads and Cavaliers cantering around the wasteland. A camp has been set up with old canvas tents. Smoke rises from a campfire, and the air crackles with excited chatter that goes right through me, jangling my nerves. I squeeze Michael's arm.

'Odds fish,' he whispers in my ear.

There are even parties of kids from other schools in our area. I think everyone for miles around has come to watch.

Bernie is setting up a burger stall; the smell of frying onions makes my belly rumble. Obo strides past, a little boy in a matching green woolly hat on his shoulders, a pretty lady in a long skirt with dreadlocks holding his hand, and I try to call out to him, but he doesn't hear me. Mr Richardson is stomping around with the megaphone, looking busy and important.

If it's none of them, well, surely there is a chance that my dad will be here *somewhere*, watching in the crowd.

We gather around Mr Samuels.

'Make me proud,' he says. 'It's been a pleasure teaching you, and this reenactment and the pageant are my goodbye presents to you all. Miss Radlett is coming back next term, so I shall be leaving.'

Everyone groans. Michael, Craig and even Kyle all look as if they're going to actually cry and I fill from top to toe with heavy sadness as I think about another person leaving me.

'Oh, don't leave, sir!'

'Please stay!'

'We'll miss you, sir.'

'We love you, sir!' my class cry out.

'If we give Miss Radlett stress again will you come back?' shouts Michael.

Everyone laughs, but Mr Samuels looks stern and

says, 'I trust you'll show kindness to Miss Radlett, and remember she's a human being with feelings, not just your teacher.' Then he smiles. 'I'm going to miss all of you too.'

With that, a Cavalier leads a beautiful black horse up to Mr Samuels, who mounts it and rides away. Mr Richardson walks up to us to chaperone, and I'm sure he gives me a special smile.

'Are you all right, Nell?' asks Miss Petunia.

I swallow. 'Yes, miss.'

There's a hush as Felicity Cordour announces over the microphone, 'Let the Celebrate Heritage Day commence.'

Everyone cheers.

Miss Petunia leads us up to the side of a roped-off area to watch the reenactment.

'Ladies and gentlemen,' Mr Richardson calls on the loudspeaker, 'Let me take you back in time to when King Charles the second was a youth and England was in the midst of a Civil War. The Battle of Naseby started on a foggy morning on June the fourteenth 1645.'

The drummer soldiers bang their drums and my heart pounds with the beat.

As both armies line up for battle the crowd

crackles with excitement.

With the war cry, 'For the king and the cause and the church and the laws,' the Royalist cavalry, led by a man playing Prince Rupert, gallop as the infantry march towards the red-coated Roundhead new model army.

The crowd cheer and the battle begins and the noise is proper deafening. Sir had told us in class what was going to happen but, no word of a lie, it's better than any words could have painted. But all I can think about is what Michael and I are about to do.

I want to stand on my head but someone might rob my oranges. I dodge away from my class, and have a little wander round where a market of olden times tradespeople has been set up. I visit the blacksmith and the printer, and watch the barber (who was also the surgeon in those days) pretend to cut off someone's leg, but the pretend blood makes me feel sick, and my basket of oranges is heavy. All the while, in the background I hear battle cries as cannons explode and the smell of gunpowder and burning sulphur fills my nostrils.

Before I know it, I hear the Royalist drummers beating the signal for retreat, and my heart beats to a crescendo. As the battle draws to a close, the crowd applauds. I push through the people to take my place at the front of the pageant as Mr Richardson says over the loudspeaker, 'Ladies and gentlemen, we're now going to bring you forwards in time from the Battle of Naseby in 1645. It's 1664 and King Charles II is on the throne. Welcome to Restoration England. Please take your places for the pageant.'

'Good luck, all of you,' says Miss Petunia, who's clipping back Tanya's blue fringe so it doesn't show under her Cavalier hat.

I turn round to check Michael's behind me. I put down my basket of oranges and am just straightening his wonky wig when Craig Boswell, dressed as Samuel Pepys, shoves us both out of the way, whacking us with his giant diary, to get to the front of the pageant.

'Samuel Pepys,' hisses Miss Petunia, 'get in your place this minute.'

I give Craig Boswell one of my *don't mess with me* looks. If you ask me it's a travesty; he can hardly write his name, let alone a diary.

But as I look at the rest of my class, all dressed so fine as ladies and gentlemen of the Restoration, as I drink in all the rich golds, purples, reds and silvers of the dresses, masks and hats with feathers and ruffles and lace, my heart pierces my soul. I want my mum. I want Mum to see this so badly.

'*I am here with you, my Nelly nell nell,*' whispers *Mum in my heart.*

I swallow and turn around to face the front.

The most enormous crowd lines the route of the pageant.

'Oranges, who wants one of my sweet oranges?' But it comes out as barely a whisper.

'*You be pretty witty Nell, smile your pretty smile, point your pretty feet and dance a jig for your crowd, as you give them your sweet oranges. That's it, you hold your chin up now. Do it for your ma,*' says *Nell Gwyn.*

And I do.

'Oranges, who'd like one of my sweet oranges?' I yell and I dance along at the front of the pageant, giving my oranges to the crowd, as I hold my head up high. I know my mum is here with me in my heart, and she always will be, and I know from somewhere back in history Nell Gwyn's with me every step of the way.

Sasha and Finn wave at me from the crowd. Then I see Willem and Gracie on the other side. TJ and

Aunty Lou are ahead of me, with Mary in her wheelchair, Tutty on her lap. I run to pat the little dog, the crowds cheer.

Old Mary looks straight into my soul and mutters under her breath, ''Tis time.'

She knows what I am about to do! Michael scoops Tutty up under his arm, shouting to the crowds.

'Behold, I am the king of England,' and the cameras flash, taking photos of the king and his little spaniel. I smile and dance my jig. The TV cameras are filming us. I blow a kiss to TJ, who's filming on his phone.

'Oranges, who wants one of my sweet oranges.'

I turn to see Michael striding behind me, smiling at his subjects, every part the king of England.

We're nearly at the youth club.

'Now,' says Michael, and grabs my hand.

I throw down my basket of oranges; they roll everywhere. I stumble over one on to my knees and Michael hauls me up. I hitch up my skirts and run to the scaffolding. Michael's already halfway up. I pull myself up after him. People are cheering, thinking this must be part of the pageant.

I reach the wooden platform and do a handstand against Michael. I feel his hands grab my ankles as he lifts me upside down over the edge.

There's a gasp from the crowd.

Then Michael shouts in his most kingliest voice, 'UNLESS ONE OF YOU GENTLEMAN CLAIM THIS FAIR MAIDEN NELL AS YOUR DAUGHTER, I, CHARLES II, KING OF ENGLAND, WILL DROP HER . . .'

Only he does . . .

32

Voices getting nearer and nearer. My head hurts. All of me hurts. Flickering lights.

I open my eyes. Lots of people round my bed. Dry mouth.

Aunty Lou holds mango juice to my lips. Her lips praying, wiping my face with a flannel. She's crying.

A nurse smiles.

For a split second I look for Mum, then I remember.

Aunty Lou strokes my cheek.

Mr Samuels is in the corner, dressed as a Cavalier. Odds fish! It all floods back.

I see Michael sitting on a chair, still dressed as King Charles, his wig wonky, looking completely terrified.

'I dropped you, Nell,' he says. 'I didn't mean to. You just slipped.'

'Michael, it's all right. It's my fault. I talked

you into it.'

I take a deep breath and gather every little drop of courage to ask the question.

'Did anyone run forward to catch me?'

Michael shakes his head.

'Anyone in the crowd claim me?'

He shakes his head again.

'Were we on TV?'

Michael nods. 'While you were out cold.'

'No one,' I say, my future cracking into a thousand pieces.

'I'm so sorry, Nell,' he says. 'No one ran forward to catch you.'

'Michael, what are you talking about?' says TJ. 'The whole estate ran forward to catch her. A whole army of Cavaliers and Roundheads ran forward to catch her. So many people ran forward!'

'Nell, listen to me, child,' says Aunty Lou. 'We all love you so, so much. You bring richness and joy to all of our lives. We are your family.'

Old Mary's words dance into my heart. 'Sometimes what we seek lies with us all along.'

And I know with every breath in my body, she's right. No word of a lie, if I'm pure truthful with myself, I know that those dad clues were desperate, flimsy cobwebs in the wind. A promised shelf, the offer of free chips, a shared Beyoncé concert, a rescued spider and a purring cat. Three men who showed kindness to me but it doesn't mean that they are my dad. And if my dad was going to come forward, he would have done so years ago. I think I just needed to play this game with myself, to keep on hoping, to somehow feel in control of the chaos Mum caused in my life. I try to say this, but no words come.

'There are photographers pushing and shoving outside the hospital to get your picture,' says Aunty Lou. 'This story will be everywhere, your picture will be everywhere, and who knows, maybe your father *will* come forward, but you need to be very grown up about this, because there must be a very good reason why your mum hasn't told you who he is. Maybe he's not the kind of person your mum wants you to have in your life. She knows that she's caused enough chaos without a dad causing more.'

I nod, swallowing the tears back. 'Or maybe she doesn't know who he is,' I whisper.

Aunty Lou takes my hand. 'It could be, child,' she says.

Michael puts his head on the pillow next to mine, his wig tickling my cheek, and we link thumbs.

'Or your dad could be an astronaut,' says Michael.

'Or a deep-sea diver,' I say.

'Or the tallest man in the world,' says Michael.

'Or the shortest,' I say.

I look into the eyes of Michael, my friend, my soulmate, my brother.

My mouth feels as dry as the desert.

'I'm so thirsty,' I say. I try to sit up.

'Michael, move,' says Aunty Lou, and she adjusts my pillows and helps me sit up, holding the beaker of sweet mango juice to my lips.

I look into Aunty Lou's eyes.

I know I must ask the hardest question of all. I take a deep breath.

'Am I going to get sent away?' Fear gips my belly.

Aunty Lou shakes her head.

'Not if you will have us. Your mum's going to take a long while to get strong again and she needs the time away at the rehab and everything they have to offer her to start her recovery. She's made it very plain to children's social care that she would like you to stay with us. And they're happy with that, so I am to become your official guardian. No one will ever replace your mum but we would all very much like to be your family.'

'And my animals' family too.'

'Yes, we will be your animals' family too. All are welcome, even Aunty Lou the hamster,' she says, laughing.

'I'm honoured to call you my little sister.' TJ winks and sits on the edge of the bed. 'So honoured that I am even willing to share a room with Michael so that you can have your own bedroom.'

He takes his old phone out of his pocket. It's in a new orange phone case, with a red and yellow parrot on it.

'For you, Nell,' he says. 'Welcome to the family.'

'So this means I'm your big brother too?' Michael pipes up. 'Cos I'm two months, three days older than you. Does that mean that I can tell you what to do now?'

'Michael, that day will never happen,' I say.

Everyone laughs.

I look round at them all. Aunty Lou cares about me as much as any mother could, and TJ and Michael are the best brothers anyone could ever have.

I close my eyes. I know this wasn't my plan but, no word of a lie, I think it's the best thing that could have happened. I have a whole family to catch me.

'Thank you, Nell Gwyn,' I whisper.

I open my eyes and peep through my lashes.

Mr Samuels is holding Aunty Lou's hand and she's smiling into his eyes, and he doesn't look faded any more. Maybe my plan has worked, maybe my family will get a dad after all.

There's a clattering at the window. A white dove perches on the window sill, peeping into the room at us, cooing, and he has a twig with a white rose and a green leaf in his beak.

Aunty Lou smiles. 'Angels in heaven, look at that dove,' and then she says words from the story of Noah's ark in the Bible:

'*The dove returned to him towards evening and there was a freshly plucked olive leaf in its beak. Noah then knew that the water had subsided from the earth.*'

In the end, I know that my animal family, Asbo and Chaos, Fiz and Tyrone and Aunty Lou hamster, Bob Marley and me are home for good.

From the shadows in the corner Nell Gwyn smiles, and takes her curtain call. She whispers, 'Thank you and good night, my pretty Nell,' blows me a kiss, curtsies and vanishes.

ORANGE HOUSE
REHABILITATION
Yorkshire

Dear Nell,

I've the picture of you with the mayor on my bedroom wall. I look at it every day. I'm so proud to be the mother of the only naturalist on the Beckham Estate.

It means a lot to me that you go to your meetings with other children of alcoholics and that you have a safe place to talk about your feelings. The outings you go on sound like lots of fun. I know that you'll have lots of facts to tell the other kids when you go to the safari park next week!

The Orange House Rehabilitation Programme is extraordinary. I can feel myself getting stronger and my mind clearer as I go for long walks on the Yorkshire Moors.

I'm working towards becoming a mentor, so that I can reach out and help someone else start on their road to recovery.

We have therapy in the Orange Room, where I talk about how I don't deserve a daughter like you but I must learn to forgive myself before I can move on. There's actually a painting of Nell Gwyn on the wall, carrying her basket of oranges. I could've sworn she winked at me the other day.

I cannot wait for you to come and visit me next week with Aunty Lou, and guess what? You'll meet a white horse, like in our special rhyme. His name's Raphael, after the angel, and he's *my* angel, helping me get stronger and to take one day at a time, without having a drink.

Nell, I hope in time you'll forgive me.

I wish nothing but good things for you, my darling daughter. I love you so very much. I'm nothing without you.

As you drift off to sleep at night, picture your mum on a white horse, with rings on her fingers and bells on her toes, riding through your dreams.

Your loving undeserving mum Xxx

P.S. Please give love to Fiz and Tyrone, Aunty Lou the hamster, Beyoncé and Destiny, Asbo and Chaos, and Bob Marley from me.

Curtain Call

Applause and gratitude to Naomi Greenwood, my oh so patient, visionary editor, for pushing and guiding me to find the story within the vivid world I saw in my head. Jodie Hodges, my one in a million agent and her assistant Emily Talbot, who held my hand throughout. Also thanks to Jane Willis and Molly Jamieson at United Agents for all you do. Hodder Children's Books, thank you for having the foresight to allow me to tell this story, Michelle Rochford for your sublime cover and Rebecca Logan, my amazing publicist for her support, kindness and wisdom.

For all things Nell Gwyn: The story of Nell Gwyn by Peter Cunningham was a valuable source of information. Kate Butterworth for meeting me in St Martin-in-the-Fields where Nell Gwyn is laid to rest, and sharing your costume expertise with me. Jane Atkinson for the wonderful production of *Playhouse*

Creatures you directed at The London Studio Centre and for so generously sharing your knowledge of Nell Gwyn that day when we bumped into each other in the middle of Sainsbury's, with everyone tripping up to get past us! Kristina Macdonald from the Heinz Archive and Library and all the staff from the National Portrait Gallery.

It's been amazing walking in the footsteps of Nell Gwyn and getting a sense of who she was. Thank you Katherine Ives for giving me such a wonderful tour of Lauderdale House and for showing me Nell Gwyn's bath. Thank you to Danielle Waldman for your help that day at the National Gallery and for guiding me towards Tring Park School for the Performing Arts, which is in the house where it is said that Nell visited the king, and sharing the myth that if you hold your breath and run round the monument three times you will see her ghost!

My day at Tring Park is a treasured memory. I would like to thank Karen Fotheringham for organising my trip so beautifully. Mike Hutchinson for giving me such a fascinating historical tour and for sharing your vast knowledge with me and the principal Stefan Anderson for making me so welcome. Stefan, your pupils do you credit. Alison Kenney,

Hilary Davies and Joanne Blyghton from the Westminster Archives, thank you for your invaluable help. Andrew Marcus, thank you so much for inviting me to the museum of London's wonderul *Fire! Fire!* exhibition where much useful research was gained.

With special thanks to Alistair North of Sir Marmaduke Rawdon's Regiment of Foote, part of the English Civil War Society.

For all things naturalist: I am really grateful to Ciara Farrell from the Kennel Club Library for educating me on the history of the Cavalier King Charles spaniel.

Respect and thanks due to vet Duncan D'Arcy-Howard and the Beaumont Sainsbury Animal Hospital from whom I learned so much, both during the treatment of my late cat Larry and from the wonderful animal events they hold at the practice in the evenings.

Also big thanks to vet Louise Allum, from whom I gained so much knowledge about dogs when judging with her at Dogs Trust Harefield Fun Day. Thank you to Richard Moore the manger and Natasha Bajwa the education officer for your support with all things Staffie!

Thank you Chris for taking the photograph of me

with Shireen at Dogs Trust for the back cover of the book.

I gained a lot of information from the TV programme *Vet on the Hill* with vet Scott Miller and special thanks to senior veterinary nurse Nathan White for talking to me about Hermann's tortoises.

For all things cat: Big thanks to both Cats Protection and Celia Hammond Animal trust, with special thanks to Elizabeth who volunteers at Celia's and who fostered my cat Larry, before I adopted him, and showed both of us such support in the last months of his life.

Hilary McKay, thank you for your tadpole knowledge and your mashed-up peas recipe to feed them, but most of all thank you for your kindness, encouragement and wisdom.

Sarah Todd Taylor for sharing your guinea pig knowledge.

A big thank you to Superintendent Simon Osborne from the RSPCA for taking the time to talk to me.

For all things Jamaican and culinary: Semsem Kuherhi for the years of sharing stories of your childhood in Jamaica with me and how you used to climb high up in the mango trees. Marcia Mantack, who is such a talented baker, for answering the question, 'If your mum packed a picnic hamper what would be in it?' with such imagination. Love also to her mother Pearl. Aunty Vie for sharing stories of her life with me and a special thank you to Sharon D. Clarke MBE, for telling me the story, years ago, of taking a lava lamp to bits and not being able to put it back together, which became the inspiration for Michael.

To my fellow authors, Steve Antony, Kristina Stephenson and Christopher William Hill for cheering me on to the finishing line. Special thanks to Lou Kuenzler for your support, help and good sound advice, for the times when I couldn't see the wood from the trees, and thanks to my mum Jenny Elson and my cousin Sally for her support. Thanks also to my friend Tracey. And to Paul and his wife, Claire.

Adrian Ramagge, thank you for creating my author presentations and for coming to my aid with my computer emergencies! Also thanks to Suzanne Tugwell from The College Practice, who came to my aid when my internet crashed!

For all things emergency service.

Doctor Emily Randles, Curtis Ashton and John Nyack (Kentish Town Fire Station).

Thank you to Calum Best for your brave and

truthful interviews, documentary and book about your father, George Best.

A special thanks to the team behind *Brought Up By Booze* for Children in Need, a huge inspiration for me writing this book.

This book was in true Restoration style, written partly in coffee houses. Thanks to Café Nero Kentish Town for your help with my computer and of course for supplying me with caffeine, especially thanks to Aleksandra Gazdziol and Steveo F. Gentile, and I would like to thank Sabrina Camponeshi from Pret, who always had a coffee, a kind word and a smile waiting for me on those marathon writing days!

This book could not have been written without Mr Saurabh Jain, who operated on my eyes and let me see again.

The last curtain call encore has to go to Nell Gwyn herself, one of the first actresses and trailblazer for the theatre as we know it today.

Thank you and good night.

Will You Catch Me? has a lot of love and laughter, but sadness too.

For many of you it will just be a moving story, but for those of you whose lives are affected by a parent or relative with an alcohol addiction remember the Six 'C's:

I didn't **cause** it
I can't **control** it
I can't **cure** it
I can take **care** of myself
I can **communicate** my feelings
I can make healthy **choices**

Nell is extremely fortunate in that she has Aunty Lou to talk to and such a good friend in Michael.

Some of you may feel like you don't have any one to talk to but please remember you are not alone.

The National Association for Children of Alcoholics (Nacoa) has a helpline:

0800 358 3456

You can call to talk to someone in confidence at any time.

The ***Orange House Rehabilitation Programme*** in my story is not real, but there is help out there for people who want to stop drinking – but remember, the adult has to want to do that themselves. Remember the Six 'C's above and look after yourselves.

Love to all my readers,
Jane Elson

More about Nell Gwyn:

It is said that everyone who researches the life of Nell Gwyn, ends up in total awe of her. In my experience it's true – what a woman! My lasting impression of Nell is as a clever, witty trailblazer. Before King Charles the second (known as the Merry Monarch) reinstated theatre after Oliver Cromwell closed them for eleven long years, men played the parts of women. Nell Gwyn became one of the first professional actresses in England, blazing the path for actresses and theatre as they are today.

I cannot remember a time when I did not know the name of Nell Gwyn, her name woven into the tapestry of time.

Nell Gwyn, worked as an Orange Girl in the Kings Theatre that now stands on the sight of the Theatre Royal Drury Lane. She sold oranges in a basket covered with vine leaves during plays. The Orange Girls would often act as messengers between the ladies on the stage and the gentlemen of the audience. Drury Lane has always been synonymous with theatre but also crime. It divides the rich from the poor in Covent Garden, and still does so.

I was humbled to learn that Nell Gwyn was only thirteen when she worked as an Orange Girl. Her huge personality soon caught the attention of actor Charles Hart who saw her acting potential and trained her as an actress for the stage. By the age of only fourteen she was part of the Kings Company, performing at the Kings Theatre under manager Thomas Killigrew. The actresses were always addressed as 'Mrs'. There was Mrs Cory, who was cast in comedic old woman roles, Mrs Knep, Mrs Hughes, a Mrs Ann Marshall and her sister Mrs Rebecca Marshall – who Nell Gwyn was always feuding with, which must have caused a lot of dressing room dramas! Nell was known as Mrs Ellen Gwyn and the plays took place at three o'clock in the afternoon, when it was still light as they had no electricity. Nell's first recorded performance was in Dryden's *Indian Emperor*. The playwright Dryden was so enamoured by her talent that he wrote parts especially for her.

To be part of an acting company doing continuous plays must have been a wondrous thing. I would love to go back in time and watch her perform and discuss how she approached her roles.

I would like to revisit the rags part of Nell's 'rags to riches' story. I said earlier that Drury Lane was synonymous with theatre and crime and that it still is. As I walk down Drury Lane today, what saddens me is the amount of people that I pass, slumped in the street, due to alcohol or other addictions.

Nell Gwyn would have seen a similar scene as she made her way home from the theatre, but Nell Gwyn's mother, Old Ma Gwyn was an alcoholic, so she had even more to deal with when she got home. Old Ma Gwyn eventually drowned whilst drunk in a ditch near Westminster.

Samuel Pepys records seeing Nell Gwyn in the doorway of her lodgings at the *Cock and Pie* pub, at the bottom end of Drury Lane where she lived whilst working as an actress. But when she was an Orange Girl, she would have gone home to Cole Yard Alley, at the top end of Drury Lane, to her drunken mother. What would that have felt like? Fast forward to today. The statistics are shocking. They reckon one in five children has a parent with an alcohol problem. The seeds for my children's novel *Will You Catch Me?* were sown.

As an author, I believe that every child has the right to see their story reflected in a book. Heroes and heroines that they connect with, who might give them the courage to speak out about what's happening at home.

Obviously being a dyslexic actress, and now an author, has its challenges. Nell Gwyn could not read or write, yet managed to perform in fifty plays a season. I would so love to ask her: how did you learn your lines? *How?* How did you even do that?

She always signed herself EG, as she could not write Eleanor Gwyn.

So EG, I salute you with love, awe and respect for the path you blazed for actresses and for women.

JE